BLACK MARINA

also by Emma Tennant

THE COLOUR OF RAIN
(under the pseudonym Catherine Aydy)

THE CRACK

THE LAST OF THE COUNTRY HOUSE MURDERS

HOTEL DE DREAM

THE BAD SISTER

WILD NIGHTS

ALICE FELL

QUEEN OF STONES

WOMAN BEWARE WOMAN

THE ADVENTURES OF ROBINA

for children

THE BOGGART
(with Mary Rayner)

THE SEARCH FOR TREASURE ISLAND

THE GHOST CHILD

ff

EMMA TENNANT

Black Marina

faber and faber
LONDON · BOSTON

First published in 1985
by Faber and Faber Limited
3 Queen Square London WC1N 3AU
This edition first published in 1986

Typeset by Goodfellow & Egan Ltd., Cambridge
Printed in Great Britain by
Whitstable Litho Ltd., Whitstable, Kent

The line on page 108, 'They fuck you up, your mum and dad', from Philip Larkin, is reprinted by courtesy of Faber and Faber Limited. The quotation from Alice Walker on page 127, from *Meridian*, is reprinted by courtesy of the Women's Press

British Library Cataloguing in Publication Data

Tennant, Emma
Black marina.
I. Title
823'.914 [F] PR6070.E52

ISBN 0-571-13939-6

for
Anne Wollheim
in memory of Gurty Owen

ADVERTISEMENT

The tiny island of St James in the eastern Caribbean forms a link in the chain which stretches from Tobago to Dominica. At a latitude of 120° – and rumoured, incidentally, to have been the real setting for Daniel Defoe's *Robinson Crusoe* (or so the locals insist over the scrumptious rum punch) – Trinidad is just a seaplane-hop away. Four miles to the north-east of wooded Grenada with its ancient fortress and fabled spices, St James is one of the more exclusive types of resort. Long white beaches that look like no one's walked there since Man Friday. A lagoon and primeval jungle. And a truly stunning hotel, where all the most evocative features of the old plantation house are blended with a luxury that's bang up to date. Choose your own *mousseline de fruits de mer* by the pool. Or select callalloo, a sancoche or a roti – just some of the exotic and intriguing Caribbean dishes on offer. Whatever you do choose, you've no choice but to accept the peace and tranquillity.

Here's our recipe for that punch:

Standard golden rum (as much as you like). Booster of white rum (watch out there). Grenada nutmeg (pow!). Angostura bitters, the mythical aromatic concoction of gentian and other herbs and spices. Fruit juice and water (don't drown it).

And if you're one of those super-executives who are contemplating Christmas on the magical island of St James, here's the recipe for the St James traditional Christmas punch. The Island's legendary non-alcoholic blender with rum is sorrel. Dried sorrel sepals are infused with cinnamon, cloves, sugar and orange peel. Leave for two or three days and then strain. The drink is a pleasant red colour, with a fresh spicy taste. Book early for Christmas!

AFTERNOON

Her head came in like a blot on the water – like a drowned spider – and I wouldn't have seen her in the first place if it hadn't been for the helicopter with its whirring over the island just at the hottest time when all the white people rest.

The noise drew me out of the store. Thank the bloody Christ I'll be away from here soon. That's me, pick up me cutlass an me three-cornered hat and go. 'Where you going next, Holly?' they say at the Coconut Bar when the nutmeg's run out and the brown rum makes puddles on the counter. 'South China Seas again, eh?' 'Our favourite lady pirate' – and all that. But it's not funny any more. The cutlass can well come in handy. And I'm not leaving this godforsaken island until the pistol arrives from the US of A. 'Mind they don't drop it in the sea near Cuba, Holly,' Jim Davy said down at the bar that night – but then he went too.

There was a big yacht moored out beyond the bar, to the left of the store and straight in my line of vision, framed by a couple of palms and Mighty Barby doing press-ups (in this heat) on the beach. But there's nothing so strange about that. This time of year is high season. They reckon, I daresay, that trouble's over for the meantime. That's an American chopper, like a bee gone off course from its pollen trail at the lip of Grenada, just four miles away. Maybe, for all I know, the people on the yacht like the sense of security it gives – tearing blades, high security, police presence and all. You might not think it was much of a holiday. But – again maybe – it's the only safe holiday you can have these days if you're stinking rich.

The girl must have climbed off the yacht when I was still in the store, counting out change for Mrs Van der Pyck. (A big dinner party last night up at Carib's Rest: snapper and lobster ordered from the fishermen days ago, mangoes – but the old ketch, the *Singer*, didn't come in this morning; a storm blew up last night and there's no mango after all. 'Holly, give me some of that terrible artificial ice-cream.') The girl, as I say, was just a head at first – it could have been a coconut, blown off in last night's winds. Or, when you began to see the tentacles of hair trailing, a big, bobbing, bad-luck black widow spider. And let's say that's what she proved to be. I had no evidence yet, and no evidence to the contrary either. But she looked like bad luck to me.

The island of St James used to belong to the Allard family. The family was split into two branches – the elder had a house at the north end of the island and the younger, three miles away at the southern tip, sat out on its wooden terrace above the lagoon and there was nothing to see until you got to South America. Not that they ever did, of course. The Allards had intermarried for generations and were far too tired to go to Trinidad, let alone Venezuela or Nicaragua. Their money came from Trinidad, anyway. A seventeenth-century Allard had made a fortune in arrowroot, and then there was sugar, always sugar, and slaves. Life on St James was – and still is – pretty feudal. The first time I came here, taken by my friend Teza, I thought Russia in the days of the serfs must have been like this: those big estates, and the trees, and a gentle wind always blowing, while the money and the sale of human sweat takes place somewhere else. In the case of St James there's a small village at the top of the hill (the island looks like a child's drawing of a whale) and a cottonhouse, for there used to be a small crop of Sea Island cotton.

When I went to St James with Teza, the descendants of the slaves were sitting on the cottonhouse floor, picking cotton.

They were all women, and the voice of Martin Luther King came out of a transistor on the stone floor with a metallic, melancholy sound. I remember thinking the words and music must mean as little to the women as the voice of some rare species of tree frog, swum over from the botanical gardens the circumnavigators loved to plant on the island, near the edge of the sea. I was wrong, as it turns out.

It was very hot – the rainy season – and the mangrove swamps below the cottonhouse had a sort of pall of mist rising up over them. If there was any sign of life at all it would be one Allard visiting another, going along the narrow dirt road like a fly. By the time I went, they had jeeps; but I used to laugh, thinking of the Allards in the old days, crawling back and forth along this track, with offers of marriage and candied fruits, in a pony and trap. Then, the three-and-a-half-mile length of the island must have taken quite an hour to do. Maybe they rested the horse by Man o' War beach, where the big rollers come in on the windward side. And by the time they arrived at the house at the southern tip of St James, the inevitable face of cousinship and interbreeding could have seemed at least a little removed.

When Teza and I went all that time ago to St James (I was bar-hopping, working as barmaid all over the States, and Teza was a journalist) the car that crept along the dirt track towards us was one of those giant-size American cars, a Cadillac probably, or a Pontiac about ten years old, and there was a body in the back. It was the body of the last remaining Allard, and now there were none left. The strain of the proposals and the infertile adjacent marriages had finally wiped the family out. A servant was driving old Allard to the jetty to load him on to the *Singer*. They must have kept him in the underground ice house at the northern end of the island, I suppose. Because the *Singer* only visits once a week, or did then, at least. Nowadays a few things have changed.

I never liked it here in the first place. It's the kind of thing that happens to you, and you wonder how. It's money, of course. Everything is. You take a part-time job one day in a small store on an island that looks as if someone had thrown it into the sea because they had no use for it. And there you are, still wrapping plastic reindeers and digging out the mince pies for Mrs Van der Pyck fifteen years later. Of course, some things have changed. We didn't sing carols to the sound of US helicopters in the old days. And there weren't any T-shirts with slogans printed on them, like we sell now. YANKS HANDS OFF I'll write on mine one day. But I wouldn't mind betting I'll be the one to go home first.

The girl only lifted her face out of the water a couple of times for air. I stood and watched as the dark head came up to the wooden platform they put at the Coconut Bar for those who've had a couple of daiquiris too many and fall in. She lifted her head there and stared straight at me. Her black hair was all over her face. Behind her, like a flat, badly painted canvas in this heat that distorts everything as soon as you look at it, was the yacht. No sign of life whatsoever.

The helicopter was making a terrible din. It was like a great sheet being torn up. I went outside the store and leant against a palm. Mighty Barby had finished his press-ups and gone away. There was no one between me and the scuffed sand, and those ugly pink shells the local kids find at the lagoon and try to flog to tourists at the Bar, and the blue sea nibbled by dead palm fronds – and the girl who had pushed off from the side of the platform now and was swimming in as if she'd been given my address the other side of the world and was making straight for me. And I'm not so far off the mark there, either. Except that there *was* one other figure in the landscape – coming towards us down the beach, just as she swam in.

Afternoon may be the time when white people out here have a good lie-down (and especially today with the Christmas

Eve Ball at the hotel to look forward to) but it wasn't too much of a surprise seeing Sanjay walk along the beach in this kind of heat. I'd easily not have seen him at all if the swimming blot of dark head hadn't unnerved me somehow and made me look to right and left, like an old woman trying to make up her mind whether to cross the road. (And I will be an old woman soon if I don't get off this goddamn island by New Year.) The truth is, recent events have made everyone jittery here. Even Jim Davy, just about the calmest, thickest American you're likely to meet, half jumped out of his skin the other night at the Bar when a bat flew in over the water and dive-bombed him on the skull. You keep moving your eyes from side to side – and often as not you catch another pair of eyes doing the same.

There wouldn't be any danger of that with Sanjay. I honestly don't think he knows or cares what's going on here. He walks up from the lagoon to the shop or the Bar once or twice a week in his straw hat and his white flannels with green stains at the knees and he smiles and orders a Coke or a ginger ale. He likes to talk about his garden, or about a new consignment of exotic birds he's ordered from the Far East, or whatever. He's proud of the fact that his is what he calls an 'open aviary' – the birds can leave if they wish, but most of them seem not to want to. Like you could say that about me – or any of the villagers here who toil for the bloody millionaires – I'd like to say – being sarcastic, of course. But you can't: Sanjay would look hurt. Maybe that's how the rich get away with it. They leave you with the feeling they just don't belong to this world anyway.

Not that Sanjay is fantastically super-hyper-rich. Not any more. Sometimes I think people just think he is. Because he's the last remaining nephew of the Allard family – he came out to St James when the old man died, and he stayed on. Like me, you could say. But with some difference. The house at the southern tip of the island had been derelict for years –

that branch of the family must have died out in the thirties – and no one had expected this nephew, who'd spent his childhood and youth in England, to come out and settle in St James. He had a wife then, and she died. That's why, some people say, he never got the strength to load up his things on the *Singer* and go.

Sanjay was still a white shimmer on the sand, like a line of light that's got into film and cracked the photo, when the girl came in up the beach and rolled for a moment on her back to stare up at the sky. I'd gone into the store by then, and I was pretending to wipe a frosting of tinsel, fallen off the decorations that Mrs Van der Pyck had pressed into the arms of her maid Millie, from the counter top. I could see the girl perfectly well, of course, through a pyramid of cans of concentrated orange juice, but I was pretty sure she couldn't see me. And by the time she'd picked herself up and tossed her hair to get it dry, and started to dance towards me – yes, lifting up her feet high, because the concrete walkway outside the store gets scalding hot this time of day – I'd slipped into the Craft Centre through the back door of the store. It's always nice to be near a phone, I say. And I could see her through the opening to the Centre, framed by pottery jugs hanging by their handles and bursts of raffia baskets, and I saw she's lighter-skinned, not a high yellow but definitely lighter-skinned, than I had at first thought. A pretty girl. A pretty honey colour, like a sponge. If it wasn't for her expression – I just couldn't go for that at all.

Sanjay wandered down the beach where the hedge of sea-grape trees can whip back at you if you push too hard against the broad shiny leaves – and if you don't, you're driven by the narrowness of the strand into toe-stubbing coral. By the time he passed the bamboo shelter for the millionaires to rest under, on the rare occasions they walk to the southern tip of the island, the flop of his straw hat and a lime green scarf at the neck had come into view. At one point, where the reef recedes and water shows a deeper, bluer blue, he slipped off his straw slippers and waded in, head peering down, like a seabird marking fish. Below him, shoals of guppies darted like fireworks.

Then Sanjay stood back and surveyed the island. Trousers rolled up, he stood in the sea up to his knees without moving, as if he half-permanently belonged there, like a merman. His tropical jacket, with its greenish, sea-lichen look, seemed a part of him too, grown on him, encrusted like a fine thing found in a wreck. He stood among and was part of the sand and water and scraggly forest in the background, the uncleared manchineel trees and the scrub that seals off the lagoon and the privacy of his creaking house.

It's impossible to imagine that by New Year Sanjay's lease runs out. After all, he was here before the rich people and the houses with ornamental gables, and the bougainvillea round the pools.

It got he was called Sanjay because he was James Allard, and when he came to St James about the time it was clear the old man was going to die, he said the place wouldn't know itself in a few years, he was going to make such improvements.

'I'm Mister St James,' he said to the visiting dignitaries from Trinidad, as he showed his latest inventions for swamp clearance, mosquito riddance, a water reservoir for the village and a new roof for the little Methodist chapel that used to make you feel when you went inside, like you're trapped in a fault of Nature: the intense blue on all sides and the roof open to more blue, and creepers growing up through the cracked stones like a beard. Sanjay – Mr St James – altered all that. He had the Allard money, of course, but he was a sixties man of money too. I think he saw the village as a sort of commune, only one that would cater pretty exclusively to his needs. What he chose to forget, it seems, was that while old man Allard had sold off the northern end of the island to a consortium of American and Venezuelan businessmen, he had only granted a lease to his nephew. Pure greed probably; it made it a better deal for him. Sanjay could indulge his dreams, while the money lasted, in the jungle of the small estate by the lagoon. He never cleared the trees there. Visitors wanting ibis or flamingo for their home movies are only allowed the near end, the stretch of water you can see from the Coconut Bar if you lean out on the rail over the sea.

Now the consortium, after the sixteen-year lease Allard had granted his nephew runs out in the New Year, will be in possession of the whole island. The major development will start. They'll pull down the wooden house. A digger and dumper will wrench out the roots of the trees – it's already started and you won't hear the trees scream over the roar of the engines. Sanjay's red cockatoos will go off into the sky. But after what's happened round here recently, why should Sanjay care? Do I care? I think about the day I first came here with Teza – when the island, from the deck of the *Singer*, looked as if it might, like a gentle whale, blow out a spout of water. It even, in that haze of heat, seemed to be moving slowly away from us like a peaceful dream you never can quite catch. And then I think of the day two months ago – red blood in the blue water and shots that sounded at first like a hailstorm on the corrugated-iron roof of the shed by the side of the store. Only it wasn't the rainy season. The spurts of red blood went into the bluer, deeper water where Sanjay is standing now; and, looking up at the sky, he sees his red birds clearing the tops of the trees and going off into the blue. But how much was he to blame?

You have to go to the past to find the seeds of trouble. ('There's Holly with her homespun philosophy again,' says

Jim Davy and whatever American cronies have come down on their three-masted schooners from Guadeloupe or Martinique. 'Tell us what to do next, Holly.' 'Have a Planter's.' I quite miss Jim, with his stiff knobbly knees. Plump, polite, talcum-scented, trying to look young in Bermuda shorts.) But maybe too they'll remember they weren't here when I was. When I came with Teza and we stood by the cottonhouse and looked down at that beat-up American car taking old Allard's body to the quay. And then went to the wooden house by the lagoon and were given tea by Sanjay and his wife, Duchess Dora as she was known. And went up to the village, before it became a model village for the new age of the St Jamesians, which was to learn how to operate a Poggenpohl kitchen for the visiting rich. Oh, long before any of that. But sure enough, the seeds of trouble were already there.

The trouble was that St James hung on in its own blue bubble of time. Everyone knew old Allard's stooped, broad back, his hawking cough, the way he blew his nose in his fingers as he drove the jeep through the wild cattle he was too lazy to round up and the mosquito-breeding swamps he was too idle to clear. It seemed old Allard had been there for ever, as long at least as the God with the blue eyes in the painting in the chapel up on the hill – and doing better than that old God, too, because Allard's house hadn't got the roof half falling off. Nothing would ever change.

Then he died and the consortium came and it did. At first, of course, no one knew about the consortium. Sanjay was a decadent and delightful offshoot of an old, interbred family. He even built a village hall, modelled on one of those pastoral dreams of paternalism you find in the West Country in England, and a children's zoo, where he planned to put rabbits and pigs – but the first consignment of rabbits got bitten by a mapipie snake and pigs mysteriously disappeared.

'It can come to no good,' Teza said. We were standing in

the village, which at that point was undergoing Sanjay's improvements. Open drains were in the process of being dug out. A large generator – supplying the first electric light to a people whose slave forefathers, sullen and surly all day, had turned in the light of lantern and fire to fantastic story-telling, dancing, throwing off shadows as vast as trolls on the hut walls – hummed deafeningly a few feet away. The child-ren's zoo, which had already become a kind of rubbish dump for old bicycle tyres, patches of material, torn cement bags, had a mass of small children crawling about on it. A young man was walking down the street towards us, with a transis-tor radio dangling from his wrist. Yes – I wouldn't forget that.

'His heart's in the right place,' I mumbled, meaning Sanjay and his optimistic plans to pull St James in one leap from Neanderthal to Now. 'I mean it's better to be comfortable than to die of agonizing disease in poverty!'

Those were the days when I still bothered to say that kind of thing. These days I just shrug. Who's the one who went back to England and came into money from her mother or someone and pursued her radical journalism and bought a nice little house in Portobello Road, where the West Indians are, move along, move along, please, up the Harrow Road as the area becomes more fashionable? Teza's the one. Not I. Yet you could say I was the lazy one not to go back with her in the first place. And take instead this 'temporary' job – with the tins of Carnation milk and frozen shark steak in the fridge. 'It's the most extreme form of patriarchal imperial-ism,' Teza said, and the subject was closed. But I may be a bit of a snob, I'd liked my tea on that wooden verandah where the rocking chairs groan like *Gone with the Wind* and a soft trade breeze blows through night and day, bringing a smell of fried yam from the kitchen. I didn't even mind Sanjay, I knew that worried look he had from when I used to hang round Chelsea, working in the antique hypermarkets or serving Tom Collinses at the Green Velveteen Club. The look is bloated and pinched at the same time: the effect of too much money and too much drugs and what you rip off with one hand you give munificently with the other. Just the opposite of Teza's look, I must say, and it's no surprise they didn't hit it off at all. I could see Sanjay thinking Teza the most bloody awful little puritan he'd come across in a long time.

Teza is half Czech and she has wide cheekbones and long, corn-coloured hair like a woman in a Soviet agricultural poster. But somehow she's not beautiful: her eyes are too small, they're like pieces of fossil chipped off a rock and set in a slanty angle to her nose. Which, in turn, is long and pointed, as if she's forever on the point of truffling out some unpalatable fact. And she is. She finds corruption at each step. I've laughed, sitting in my room by my hurricane lamp. (The famous electricity never reached the conglomeration of squalid houses where people like me live – misfits, white trash, old-young – missing persons who ran away from home a generation ago and are ageing here very gently, presumed dead.) I've laughed, thinking how the stallholders in Portobello Road must dread Teza, when she comes down on them with some statute or by-law she's dug up to prove they're trading illegal. Yet Teza has a kind heart, even if she does have a totalitarian mind to go with it. She keeps in touch. Last time she went to Cuba she sent me down a bundle of Havana cigars. 'It's shocking, Holly,' she said on the card from the Socialist Havana Hilton poolside. 'These cigars are still made by the women here rubbing the tobacco leaves on the insides of their thighs. And it's still a piece-work system, I'm quite surprised.' I laughed then too, smelling the warm cunt – as I liked to fantasize – of a Guantanamera woman every time I lit up a cigar at night by the lamp. Maybe those are the seeds of everything that went wrong later. For in every peach Teza must find a worm.

Looking at Sanjay, who was standing on one leg now, head craning over his shoulder backwards, posing like a flamingo in the blue water that cuts him off at the knee, I think of tea in the wooden house that day – and the picnic at the lagoon the day after. I see Sanjay must have hurt his foot or he wouldn't be standing like that, but I can't help remembering the lobster nipping him in the thick weeds of the lagoon all those years ago, and him lifting his foot and toppling in.

I laughed. I must have been mad, I suppose, because the girl in the front of the store heard me and she didn't cough or anything, she just called out, 'Who's there?' But then, through the assorted clumsy pieces of pottery that Jim Davy gets made in the new kiln in the village, I saw Millie – or half of Millie – come in the store, and the girl was quiet again. Behind the pots Millie was moving quietly about, assembling her order. What the hell does Mrs Van der Pyck want now? As if Christmas dinner and all the trimmings and a fine choice of seafood wasn't enough. Maybe it's the new people off the yacht the girl swam ashore from and I never saw them land. (It's funny here, you can so easily find you've dropped off to sleep. It's the heat.) But I'd have made a mental note of it if the minibus from Carib's Rest had come down to the jetty to pick up a load of passengers off the yacht. Maybe Mrs Van der Pyck has invited the whole island – the smart end, the northern end, that is – to dinner tonight. Well, she wouldn't ask me anyway, would she? I'm just the storekeeper here, even if the store has gone up in the world. All it used to sell was meat pies and rum – and it hired out hair clippers to Millie and other St Jamesians – in the days before the cottonhouse ever became Carib's Rest.

That first tea in the house by the lagoon, Sanjay carried the bamboo tray out to the verandah and Duchess Dora did the pouring. I'd have laughed again, if it wasn't precisely the wrong moment to do so, for seldom can so many misunderstandings have been playing themselves out in one small space at the same time. The first, and funniest, was that Sanjay's wife – I never found out why they called her Duchess Dora but it must have been something to do with her grand voice and her airs and the way she talked about huntin' in her childhood in West Ireland – anyway, Duchess D. was definitely under the impression that we were there to interview her for *Vogue* or American *House & Garden* or some such. She was even quite disappointed, I think, that I hadn't a camera – and certainly she'd dressed up in white lace for the occasion. A parasol leaned against the balustrade of the verandah, I can see it now.

'And what kind of thing do you want to ask?' Sanjay said as we sipped our tea from cups so thin they looked like those shells you can see through when they're lying in shallow water on the sand. 'You mentioned the improvements I've set in train here and I think I've filled you in about them all. The first houses for visitors will be constructed in the coming months, in the dry season, of course.' Teza's pencil pretended to race. 'And we will not, it goes without saying, alter the natural beauty of the island or imperil the ecology.' (Saving the Earth was just getting in its stride then, as the Americans blasted the leaves off the trees in Vietnam.) 'We intend to preserve an unhurried, rural way of life,' Sanjay said. He threw a quick, sharp look at Teza and I thought, he's not such a dimwit after all. The almost black hair smoothed back as if for his thousandth polo match, the slightly weak jaw, eyes that were in a mirthful, apologetic crease as if to compensate for the ridiculous luck of being an Allard less interbred than his predecessors, it's true, but rich from the money of slave owners, and knowing it. 'The conditions of the inhabitants of St James will soon be altered beyond recognition,' he said. 'By June there will be running water in the village, I'm glad to say. And the school will be fully air-conditioned!'

I'd be glad to say on this day that there's running water at The Heights, the sardonically named slum where I live, in the dip in the hill in the middle of the whale's back where no one can see us. We're not a show village – but what's the point of grumbling? Half the people there could find themselves thrown out if they make too much of a fuss.

'Will the St Jamesians be obliged to work as servants in the new hotel and wait on the winter visitors?' Teza said.

I must say, you have to hand it to Teza. But Duchess Dora came into her own at that point and saved the situation – for them, of course, not for us – in the classic fashion. The biscuit china went down with a tiny crash on the saucer; a moon face, with curls as dark as Sanjay's flat thatch and with a little-girl bandeau to hold it all in, peered in friendly confusion at her husband over the tray. 'Sanjay, darling.' The voice was meant to be lisping, but it came out hard. 'We haven't mentioned the picnic yet. We haven't invited Teza . . . and . . . er . . . '

'Holly,' I said.

'Oh, you make me think of Christmas,' this priceless woman then said. 'How divine. I was saying, we have a picnic at the lagoon on Sundays . . . children and things . . . some of the heavenly Venezuelans are coming, they're simply *camping* up at the old Allard house in the north at present . . . and you must both come . . . '

'Just a family picnic,' Sanjay said. He hadn't liked, perhaps, the mention of the Venezuelans. 'Also, I don't know where you're spending the night. But if you'd be able to bear it . . .'

'And not be put off by the *ghastly* discomfort,' Duchess Dora said.

Teza and I exchanged the most fleeting glance you could get. Mine said, why not? Teza said aloud, 'I'm sorry, Mr Allard . . . '

'Sanjay,' Sanjay said firmly. For the first time I saw he was attractive, used to getting his own way and doing it with a sudden charm out of the affectation of tiredness. He rose. His faded shirt was a very pale pink against the roaring blue of the sea beyond the posts of the verandah. Here goes, I thought, here's the photograph I was supposed to take. I decided not to include Duchess Dora in the imaginary shot (but that's me, you know – childish).

'I'd love to,' I said.

'I have a friend in the village.' Teza finally came out with her unexpected news. 'So thank you, but I've already made arrangements to stay.'

It wasn't strictly true. Teza, at her London college, had briefly known a young trainee teacher who came from St James but had gone early to live with a relative in Trinidad and then on to London on a grant: he left college and went to teach at a comprehensive in North London; he said he had a brother, much younger, on the island and Teza should look him up. But Teza is the kind of person for whom a piece of information is as solid as human flesh or a bed to sleep in. Like most people of her sort, she has no idea how much inconvenience this can cause others. And she ended up in poor Millie's bed while Millie slept on the floor – and all this just because Millie was walking with those slow, slow steps down the village street at the very moment when Teza and I, breathless in the heat from the short climb, were walking up it.

There was no shade. There were no dogs because there was no shade for them to lie in. A few chickens squawked. Out the other side of the village, down the far side of the hill, were nutmeg trees and there some old men lay. But it was too far to reach. Even the chapel, roofless, looked as if it had caved in under the weight of the blue sky. And Millie with her slow steps walked, apparently not moving, towards us. Tiers of pale washing stood on her head like a wedding cake.

A boy came out from behind one of the squat houses. He had a transistor radio dangling from one arm. We all stopped. The four of us stood there, trapped in the scene. Speed and movement-ahead to Teza and to the boy, who was still just legs-and-arms-all-over-the-place but would become Ford, the well-known, brilliant, reckless Ford. Slowness and slowness and death for Millie and me. Or that's how it seems on the afternoons when the sun's stuck up in the sky and the pyramids of cans of rock salmon are blistering to the touch, and the iced-lollie wrappers stick to the tray in the deepfreeze so the whole lot has to be melted out.

Millie never had the opportunity to move. That's why she's in the store even on Christmas Eve, pulling polythene bags of olives from what is supposed to be the cold display. 'She's so slow,' Mrs Van der Pyck says, rolling her eyes. 'But then I suppose they all are.' And as for me – where could I have gone to anyway?

Ford was Teza's friend's brother. Something had brought him out from the yard, the sound of Teza's voice probably, and my grunt of reply. He stared at the ground when Teza asked if his family could put her up for the night. And Millie said it was room in her house and she knew we'd be at the picnic tomorrow with Mr Sanjay at lagoon.

And Ford suddenly looked up at Teza and said, 'Does she want to go Coconut Bar?' And there I was. And Ford and Teza were on a moped and all the chickens ran stupidly about in the dust when they went off pop-pop-pop down the road just the way we came. Millie and I didn't look each other in the eye at all. And I walked back down again to the wooden house by the lagoon – to the irritation of Duchess Dora, who was then slap-bang in the middle of her afternoon rest.

The Coconut Bar had at that time just been put up. No lights, no jukebox, no deepfreeze for the lobster claws – just a platform out on stilts and a hat of dead coconut fronds over it. A bar, that was the nice part, an old mahogany bar Sanjay took from old Allard's house before the consortium came to see what was what. It could have been a bar in a London club, it made you think of brass fenders and fires burning and the kind of Christmas you were meant to have had as a London child (speaking for myself, I froze in an aunt's boarding-house in North Berwick). Fresh lime was kept in old lemonade bottles. The rum was stacked in a crate under the bar and new crates got hoisted in from the *Singer* with a good deal of shouting and pattering on the floor that was planks nailed together. When it got dark, there was the most spectacular sunset. Pools of crimson on a nut-brown backcloth, and sea silvery in the moon in no time, as if a toucher-up with a glitter pot hadn't had the patience to wait.

Not that I liked the nights in St James then any more than I do now. If you live in these places you just have to take the fact that the night is the one thing the white man couldn't chain down, and for all his plans and compromises he still can't. No wonder they call them *tristes tropiques*, and they don't mean the morning when the sun catches the hibiscus and a humming bird skims past and the impression is that all is made new. They mean the coming of the night. The hedge of coconut palm and seagrape along the beach go first, as suddenly as colour draining out of the cheeks of a corpse. Then the horizon, playful in the day with the outlines of small islands, is knocked flat out of the picture. It just isn't there any more. The sun splits sideways, bunging up the sky with red. This gives a blood light all over to the sand and trees – and at the same time, although there's no wind, there's a rustling, whispering sound that sounds like a whole townful of tongues. I've even heard music. I don't care what anyone says about the cruelty on these islands and the slaves beaten into silence and the long history of their mastery of the night: the dance and the tales of kings and monsters, and the song, all come out of this terrible darkness. Cane rustles, though it grows the other side of the island, over the hill, you can hear it on certain nights. It's different now in the Coconut Bar, of course. Fairy lights strung out over the sea. Music billowing deep into the waves if the sea gets up. It's all reggae and rock. You have to go to The Heights, to the crossroads of tumbledown dwellings the far side of the village, to feel that old fear and sadness now. But then, when the Bar had just been put up as a place for the few visitors to the island to call at on their way to Grenada, Carriacou, Trinidad, it's difficult to know what effect sitting there for hours on end – to a girl like Teza at least – would have had.

Sometimes I think of that evening, or rather the tail end of that afternoon, when I look at Sanjay, as I do now. (He's taken his shoe off in the water, examined the sole and replaced it: then he's wading into the shallows and his thin legs, brown as wooden stumps, are visible down to the tops of his feet.) I think how things would have been so different if Teza and I hadn't gone to St James, and if Teza hadn't gone to the Coconut Bar, and if we all hadn't gone to the picnic at the lagoon the next day. I think of Teza and Ford sitting there on the old beer crate they had for seating in those days, with the first bats of the evening diving under the thatched roof of the Bar. And flying fish making those phosphorescent trails in the water below. There's the smell of wet sand, and snappers' heads thrown into the sea under the Bar, stinking up the soft wind of the evening. Ford and Teza – they didn't exchange a word, she said – listening to the night that Ford knew everything about and Teza nothing at all. In any case, Teza flew off the next night with this so-young man with the big, quick eyes. Or rowed off, presumably. There was a fisherman's boat missing from where it had been tied up, in front of the store. You can guess who took the rap for that.

Now I just listen to the sound of that bloody helicopter. The tearing sound makes me think of the days my friend Lore and I used to go to Peter Jones and get the salesman to rip us off a yard here and a yard there in the sale, for a motley lot of cushions and curtains for our flat. That's long ago for you. And if Lore didn't write, how'd I keep up with all the goings-on in London Town? She even came out here. Barbados on a package, it was, and she came down and caught the *Singer* and put herself up in a hotel run by a Mrs Heering in St Vincent or was it Bequia? Lore's the one who knows how to get around. For all Teza's political sophistication, she's an innocent compared with Lore. And with me, I would have said in the past. But I don't know now.

We were all friends. Lore and I lived off the King's Road and worked in various bars, and Lore did a little escort agency stuff when we needed a holiday or simply a rest from serving literary drunks at the Green Velveteen. Teza lived near Westbourne Grove, Portobello Road, that area, where, as Lore put in her first letter, 'There are so many West Indians already that one more won't make any difference.' She wasn't as astonished as I was by Teza going off suddenly with Ford. I suppose nothing seems surprising in London, whereas the village here in St James did seem too remote for it to be possible for anyone to leave, let alone elope from. (This is silly, I know, because Ford's brother had already got away and is a London teacher.) Maybe it's to do with Ford's peculiar look of innocence – he could have been a child in those days, and by my standards today that's just what he was. I reckon Ford was rising eighteen that summer and Teza was twenty-two, the same age as me. And all that sixteen years ago. You could hardly blame me for failing to see the Ford-who-became-a-famous-poet, the Ford of Black Power and the final, anarchic Ford in that short day and a half before Teza took him away.

Sanjay was the first to welcome Ford-the-uninvited-guest to the picnic at the lagoon on that Sunday in December. (God, I think to myself, sixteen Christmases later and the new houses for the winter visitors are up, the interior decorators came from New York, Mrs Van der Pyck arrived and all the cotton fluff was swept out of the cottonhouse and it was made gleaming and olde worlde and rechristened Carib's Rest.)

Sanjay was unpacking a hamper and he looked up and smiled at them both, and said, 'Oh hello, Ford. Come for Sunday lunch?' And I could see Teza was disconcerted. She was so determined to make a monster of Sanjay, a colonialist, capitalist warlord, and there he was knowing the name of a youth from the village, and he grinned and held out a hand that had oil on it from the salad dressing and I could see Teza could not think massa at all.

It hadn't been a very pleasant night for me at the old wooden house by the lagoon. I see now that Duchess Dora, who lived out her last years in a state of agonizing jealousy – it's a constitutional hazard for white women in the tropics, and particularly those, like Duchess Dora, with every tiny thing done for them – had it in for me from the start. 'What extraordinary things people wear nowadays' and other similar remarks throughout the evening put my teeth on edge. Sanjay didn't seem to notice; he was kindness itself to the baby-faced wife with black curls held in by a bandeau and this hard, lisping voice that was clearly put on because it was considered to be attractive. The skins of white women go green and the hair goes lank in this tropical heat. As for me, I haven't such a bad figure – Go on, Holly! – according to Jim Davy at the Coconut Bar anyway. But if I look up now at the mirror Jim Davy insisted on installing in the Craft Centre against shoplifters (who on earth would want to steal any of his bloody pots?), I see myself just as ravaged by the bloody equator as Duchess Dora, for all her whiteness and her face creams, was then.

We all went to bed early, after a meal of a dryish pork-tasting thing that Duchess Dora sharply told me was a great delicacy, for it came from Grenada, sent by Dr Gairy himself, and it was armadillo. There was coffee on the verandah, and the groaning of the wicker rocking chairs, and our three faces in the light of the old Venetian lamp. Sanjay told me of his plans for new crops on St James. 'It's eggplants in the north,' he said. 'And we may try some tobacco.' He sounded as if he couldn't make enough plans for the exotic place he had come to. But Duchess Dora sat very quiet and pale by the coffee tray. Her airs and graces had tired her out, I thought then, uncharitably.

The picnic had that same sad kind of feeling – to me anyway – as the evening before when Duchess Dora went listlessly back and forth in her chair on the verandah. It may have been the music from Sanjay's tape deck coming out over the lagoon. After all, we were in the late sixties then, and everything was rotting with sadness and protest and self-pity and loneliness. And there's something about the tropics that makes you feel so lonely anyway. But that's just me again with my left-out feeling – for I could see Teza smile at Ford, and soon she was lying right up close to him on the rug on the sand, while Duchess Dora pouted with disapproval and Sanjay poured us rum and sliced open coconuts for the chaser.

I remember there was a sort of little creek at the side of the lagoon farthest from the house. Cinnamon trees and tall palms shielded it from view. Sanjay took me there. 'This is my favourite place, Holly,' he said. And he took my chin in his hand and held my face as if trying to decide whether or not to add a finishing touch. 'You're a lovely girl, Holly,' he said.

This, I can tell you, is par for the course. Married men, and they tell you later why they won't be able to see you after all. I can tell the dudes who come off a yacht for a bit of fun in one glance, and I can count the number of drinks they'll need before they say there's nothing doing. But the profits swell the till, and the Bar is lumped in with the store, so it all adds up. At least it used to before I looked in the accounts book last week and my eyes nearly jumped out of my head. 'Holly, you should put more water with it,' I said. But there the figures were.

If I remember fuzzily, it's because it gets on my nerves to look back to that day at the lagoon, with Sanjay holding my face and then turning away as if he was angry with himself – and so I think, only think, some small kids appeared, paddling in the creek. Yes, I guess they must have, because there was a sudden burst of rain and they all screamed and Sanjay squatted down near them. I remember noticing his broad back. His smooth hair wasn't so smooth that day, and it was falling in his eyes, so he didn't look so much like a polo-playing, wife-murdering Englishman. He'd made a small pier that stuck out into the creek and there was a model boat tied up there. The kids – now I see them, about five or six of them, white and pale brown and blackest black, and heaven knows how many of them with Allard blood from the old slave days, and Barby, the albino Negro from The Heights, just a tiny boy then with a white frizz of hair and his poor skin burning so badly from the sun. There was this quick downpour of rain, as I say, and Sanjay called to the kids to come out from under the manchineel trees. They got a poison sap, and rain coming through the leaves can burn you bad. Some of them started screaming; I reckon there'd been some harm done already.

'I made this boat,' Sanjay said when the kids had scattered over his pier. 'It's a galleon, sails and all.' And he fiddled with a string and sure enough a fine set of sails unfurled.

I was in no mood, however, for model boats at that moment. On top of which I could see Duchess Dora, who had doubtless scoured the bushes at the back of the property, and the orchid house, and the open aviary very likely too, with the swooping keskidees and humming birds no bigger than a bright leaf in the thick, tropical growth. She was walking towards us, with the fixed smile of the permanently, insanely jealous and she was carrying, as if strolling on an English lawn, a pair of secateurs.

'It's for you, Dora,' Sanjay murmured. He wasn't speaking to his approaching wife, but to his daughter, who was as pale as a vanilla ice-cream and had wafer-yellow hair to match. Pandora, I can't think why they called her that. 'Dora's lovely new boat,' he said in a fond-father voice. I felt a bit sick, you'll understand. The way men rub up to a girl, make a pass at her one moment and then speak in the same voice to a child the next. It smacks of something disgusting to me.

But by this time Duchess Dora was just a few yards away. 'Sanjay!' She didn't say my name; maybe she hoped she could disappear me into the creek like a soucriant if she thought hard enough that I wasn't there. 'Sanjay, we're all longing to unpack the hamper,' she said. 'Bring Pandora with you. Millie's laid it all out on the new coral table the other side of the lagoon.'

It was a rotten shame to have to leave then really, and especially for one of those little Creole kids who was trying to totter along the pier and play with the model boat Sanjay had made for his daughter. She was so excited to see the ship with the sails up, and there was even a breath of wind, so the canvas puffed out and the ship tugged daintily at its string. But Sanjay had collapsed the sails before the poor little brat could get there. He wasn't thinking, I suppose. And Duchess Dora – did she put on speed – she leaned over that toy pier and clouted the kid on the back of the head. So it went splash into the murky water, little pink dress and all.

'Dora!' Sanjay said in quite a different tone to his wife. But I reckon that kind of thing was happening all the time, because none of the other children paid a scrap of attention.

And it was for Millie to come on those slow, heavy legs round the bend of the creek and pull the bawling creature out. I can't say I go for kids, never have, and this wasn't a particularly attractive specimen.

'Take her up to the village, Millie,' Duchess Dora said. 'And tell Tanty Grace to keep a better eye on things. You hear?'

Millie worked for the Allards then. Mrs Van der Pyck and her equally demanding régime were yet to come.

We all sat on the gnarled beach stools Sanjay had fashioned from flotsam, and tucked into the picnic in silence. It was good – roti and beef with curry and samosas and soursops and mango, which for some reason don't grow good on St James and have to come over from another island on the *Singer*, just as they were supposed to yesterday.

'I'll tell you about the Sea Island cotton I'm considering reintroducing,' Sanjay said. He kept his eyes away from me as he talked. Duchess Dora's eyes were fixed on me, though, in fury. I want to get off of here, I remember suddenly thinking then. No one listened as Sanjay talked of crops and rainy seasons and the hurricane that hit Dominica a few years ago.

Sanjay is walking along the beach, and the helicopter hovers a moment longer before turning – in the opposite direction this time, over the island where no one will look up from the village at propellers cutting into the blue sky or look after it when it has gone down towards Laughing Gull Bay. (Sometimes the pilot amuses himself, swooping right down to the sand, and last month, after a freak tide, he found what he thought was an arm or a leg sticking up out of the sand by the reef – he's used to that kind of sight by now, I suppose. It was in fact the neck of a pre-Columbian urn. 'So beootiful' – I can hear Jim Davy now, when it was brought in to him by the pilot. Wide, a warm brown, chased with pale painted whorls. 'We'll put it in the Craft Centre,' Jim Davy said. 'We'll teach the students to make an urn like that.')

I get these flashes of fear, they last as long as the shadow from a chopper's blade, and it suddenly comes to me that Sanjay is walking towards me with news of disaster. Is there a war starting up? What can he see, from the verandah of his wooden house where you can stare and stare and you won't see anything until you get to the coast of South America? He could see a fleet all right, steaming up to fight out a bloody Falklands on our beaches. But the British don't want anything to do with protecting St James. When we were made 'independent' (what a laugh), along with St Jude to the north, and a chinless member of the Royal Family came – he was trying to grow a beard, I remember, the sweat of the tropics came through the pathetic straggle of hair – what a fuss Duchess Dora made! Oh, the tea on the lawn! a steel band, even. It was embarrassing. But they don't want anything further to do with us. The fighting'll be between the Cubans and the Americans. I see it in my dreams and then the Russians fly in in planes from dark skies heavy with snow.

'Holly!' I hear. I go into the store, it's time I served Millie, after all, because her basket is full with those extra trimmings Mrs Van der Pyck needs for tonight. 'You going to dinner up there?' Millie says, and I shake my head and we both laugh. We'll be sick-drunk together later, no one is stopped from going into the Coconut Bar. In a comic-strip show of equality and comradeship, the Americans and Venezuelans will dance with the villagers from St James and the funny hats will go on and we'll all be happy as the night is long. Mrs Van der Pyck will make her annual pass at Sanjay, who will slip away before the end. Jim Davy dressed as Santa Claus. 'What are you giving us this year, Santa, to keep us good?' But Jim Davy's not here, and that's one of the reasons I suspect bad news.

Now I'm back in the store I see the girl from the yacht has an impatient look. She's swum over with a wad of dollars tucked in her hair and she's laid them out on the counter.

What is she trying to prove? And now I find there's a lump in my throat. It's fear again. Because every day this place gets more and more like a re-run of an American TV serial. I just expect her to pull a gun – and point it at me. Steady on, Holly, I say to myself as I add up Millie's shopping on the ancient cash register.

'Going away on holiday this year?' I say to Millie, to keep up the seasonal running joke between us. And Millie laughs – that slow, rumbling laugh that makes you feel quite cheered up until you remember you're stuck on an undefended island only four miles from Grenada.

'Just the usual little skiing holiday,' she says. 'In Switzerland.' And we both laugh together, while the girl stands staring at us in open contempt. A couple of old bats, you can see her thinking about us. And I think back, well, dear, you'll just have to wait your turn to get served. As if we were in one of those crummy streets in West London where you see girls looking like this one, and not on an island that might be blown up any minute and the pieces scattered as far as Trinidad.

Lore was the one who wrote and told me the news, that Christmas after Teza vanished with Ford. (They'd gone to Union Island in the fisherman's boat, it was later revealed, and had a lobster dinner and spent the night in the one battered hotel.) It was the first time Ford had left St James. By the time they got on the big plane to London in Barbados his eyes were nearly popping out of his head.

'It's cradle-snatching,' Lore said. 'But he is rather sweet. Do you know, he even writes poems and reads them aloud to Teza's friends? No one dares to laugh, of course. Teza's bought this little house near the Portobello Road. She seems quite happy, but she's restless really. Something tells me she'll have a baby next. Well, I suppose you can afford to if you get left a nice lump of money and you've got a roof over your head and you just stroll down to the market for your yam or sweet potato every time you get a crave.'

Well, yes. As for me, I stayed and I worked at first in the Coconut Bar because the store was nothing then, just for locals. Sanjay said to me, the day after Teza and Ford disappeared and he was finally sure in his mind that I hadn't aided and abetted them by pinching the boat or anything, 'Why not stay on here, Holly? We have great plans for St James, you know. You can join in the fun. You give me the feeling you've been left out, not joining in, all your life somehow.'

(It's funny what a few kind words will do.) And what did I have to go back to? A furnished room in Chelsea where you can see the river if you lean out of the window, and you feel like throwing yourself in if you could jump that far, and a religious maniac living underneath who comes up and threatens you with her Bible when the wind's easterly. And it's so warm here, the nights are as warm as swimming in your own blood when you lean on the rail at the Coconut Bar. (Not forgetting that in those days the yacht owners gave big tips. Now they have Ferdie, a great laughing man from Tobago, to mix the punch and the daiquiri.)

'You'll never believe this,' Lore's next letter went. 'I had supper round at Teza's last night' (this was some years later, I've lost count). 'Ford's in Black Power now. He has yellow socks and a navy wool cap pulled down over his head and a belt with so many spikes and studs it makes you think you're at the Tower of London. And he's a celebrity! He shouts out his poems at meetings, he raps to an astonished audience in the drawing rooms of the English literary world. Holly, it's too funny. You should come back just to see.'

Of course I did get homesick a lot, but somehow there was never the funds or the time to get home. Lore sent a photo of herself and some passing boyfriend in a grim-looking farm place where he rears chickens. She looks pretty miserable and certainly cold. Anyway, I feel as if I'm sewn into this place by now. I know St James so well that I can't imagine the streets at home any more, or the English rain, or the first strawberries in the market, with the mushy ones hidden underneath. The strange thing is, you don't feel the stitches going in. One day, though, there you are. I'm part of the needlework by now, just as much as Sanjay as he saunters along the beach, skipping the wavelets that come in over half-moon-shaped pillows of sand.

But – today – there's someone who doesn't fit at all. Swim back the way you came, my girl, I say under my breath as she fixes that long, rude stare on me. Then I see, behind Sanjay, there's another unexpected face. Damn it, I say, what an afternoon it turns out to be.

I suppose you could place Sanjay's daughter Pandora in the category of things that come and go here in St James. It was a tragic thing. But I wasn't honoured with the company of Sanjay and Duchess Dora much in those days, as Duchess D.'s discovery that I was serving at the Bar instantly put the place out of bounds for her husband. (I never knew why he put up with it. No one said, of course, when Dora died, that it must have been a relief for him, but it's hard to see how it could not have been.) But Sanjay's daughter – I remember her that day of the picnic at the lagoon when she ran from the uncleared trees to join her father – now she's all in white, in a long dress like a portrait of a Victorian girl; she's making a sound like a laughing gull, swooping in white over the sand behind Sanjay.

What happened to Pandora is hard to figure out. Mrs Van der Pyck, who is the island gossip, she says Pandora inherited madness from her mother. But then Mrs Van der

Pyck hated Duchess Dora too. (Sometimes I wonder if the poor woman's maddening air of superiority didn't get her ill-wished by so many people that she was likely to sicken and die. But one mustn't think like that in this part of the world. It's too dangerous, there's so much of it around. Maybe I should do better to bear in mind Teza's strictures on under-development and superstition in the Third World. All the same, it was mysterious that Duchess Dora died of an illness that had never before manifested itself in the Caribbean. I've felt guilty about it myself, to tell the truth, like you do when someone dies and you just couldn't care.)

Sanjay never forgave his wife for sending the girl away to the madhouse, that was the *on dit* on the island. But where else could she have stayed? You can't lock up a young girl so easily these days, even here. Some visitor or other would have talked about it in St Jude or Trinidad and they'd have come and shipped her all the way to Barbados, that's the way I see it. Whereas the asylum in Grenada is – or was – so near that Sanjay used to go once a month to see Pandora and come back looking haggard and sad and go and sit in the bar at Carib's Rest and drink brandy and water the colour of mahogany. And you could say all was well, up to a point – at least he could see her – until the Bishop revolution in Grenada and he stopped going over altogether. And then Duchess Dora went down with that fever and died. I used to feel sorry for Sanjay. So many youthful, optimistic plans, London swinging to his tune when he was just starting out, the chance to transform an island in the sun, and he ends up in a falling-down house alone, with his wife dead and his daughter out of her mind. Then the Bishop régime was overthrown two months ago and in the fighting the madhouse was bombed to the ground. There were twenty or thirty killed. Heaven knows how Pandora escaped unhurt. She was found wandering near the garrison by an American marine. Rescued – airlifted: Sanjay told Jim Davy he had a lot to be thankful for and he knew Jim Davy had pulled every string he could to help. 'I won't forget,' he said to Jim Davy every night in the Coconut Bar. I used to fall half-asleep listening to Sanjay going on and on about the saving of the life of his daughter. And I couldn't help thinking, it might have been better for her if she hadn't been saved at all. She's out of her wits, poor darling.

It wasn't long after the day of that picnic at the lagoon that little Pandora fell into madness. Millie thought someone had put a hex on the child. Her look said as much. I remember we were standing up near Corbeau Bay in the north, where the consortium was pushing ahead with the first stage of building, and Millie had gone up with sandwiches for the labourers. I was just hanging around – you can certainly get restless on a place like this. And from this point in the north you can see the big tankers on their way up from Venezuela to the USA. Sanjay would be there some days too, supervising the building with his overseer, Mr Ritchie, and pointing to the places where he wanted to put in clematis and flowering vine and frangipani.

Pandora was very subdued at the picnic, I remember, because it was the one time I wouldn't have minded some childish disturbance to cover up Teza and Ford making eyes at each other.

No one knows a thing about madness, or so it seems to me, in spite of all the theories. It probably is inherited in this case. But I'll have to admit it gave me a great fright – oh, about a month ago it must have been – when I was packing up late here at the store and I heard a terrible screaming coming from the direction of the lagoon. They've been clearing there recently, hacking down Sanjay's private jungle to make way for an airport. His lease runs out any day now, as you know.

Pandora had apparently wandered off down there, Millie said. (She'd heard this from her Tanty Grace who'd come down to the Allard house to help out with Pandora since the bombing of the Grenada madhouse.) Pandora had gone down to the little creek. The manchineel trees were half cut down and the bank had been bulldozed, so the place sort of jumped out at her, where the miniature jetty had been, and then she started to scream.

All that's as it may be. I don't like my store overcrowded. Sanjay and his daughter will be here any minute now and it just won't do at all.

'Can I help you?' I say in a surly voice to the girl while I finish wrapping black olives for Millie. (American Mediterranean! Half the visitors down here pretend they've gone to Greece, we've even had orders for retsina. They're missing the culture. There's no culture here and no history and without those you can't have a sense of achievement, or so says V. S. Nightfall.)

'Will I be seeing you later at the Coconut Bar?' I say to Millie, although of course I know I will.

And Millie says, 'I don't know if I'll make it this year.' Which is her stock reply, except I see in her eyes all of a sudden that she means it this year. And we both see together the red blood spreading in the sea and the little fishes with bulging eyes that jump in and out of the waves as if nothing on earth was going on.

'I'll see you alone,' the girl says.

Just like that. Millie stands back and looks at her in earnest and I think at the same time how the two women could have come from a different planet, for all they could ever know about each other or understand. The girl – her hair is drying out now and I see it's really quite fair, in an Afro. Her eyes, gold, yellow-gold, with flecks and curls of light. Chrysanthemum eyes. A wide face, a beautiful face if it wasn't for the expression, the mouth that's set like a strung bow, the lips that hardly part, as if she's learned from an early age not to give anything away. Her shoulders and neck are slender. Her colour is lovely, like gold, half-wet, half-dry out in the sun. Millie looks at her as if she can't see her properly, with that blind look of eyes white like sea shells in a black, black face. She turns away, shoulders thick with the muscle of a lifetime's labour. The two carrier bags are hoisted up as she turns to the door, showing a great stomach starting up high under the breasts. Then she turns back towards me.

'I do love him, Holly. Whatever he do he OK by me.' And she walks out the door, through a rattle of Polynesian beads Sanjay brought back from a tour to the South Seas in earlier, happier days. Beads and miniature conches – they rattle and shake as she goes, like the orchestra of a tribal queen. Through all this the girl stands half-on to both of us, looking at Millie through lowered lids. 'When Ford so high' – Millie's hand sweeps down – 'we play mas together.' Her mouth suddenly opens in a dazzling white grin. 'Christmas only a-sing de carols' – in self-mockery this, with a look of humorous self-deprecation; Millie is a fantastic mime. 'So what damn good Christmas this year for me?'

'Ford would want you to come and dance,' I said. But I knew my tone was insincere. Ford wouldn't have cared what Millie did, as long as she was getting re-educated away from imperialism and on to the true path.

The girl steps forwards, the swinging beads throw shadows on her tawny body and she stands there dappled like a beautiful cat. 'Ford,' she says, 'where is he?'

Ford was kind to Millie the only time she was sent over to London. Mrs Van der Pyck had organized a cooking course: Millie, who had pounded plantain with pestle and mortar like her mother and grandmother and fried yam and cooked up the fish as it came in, was to learn how to decorate a breaded veal escalope with anchovy turrets, or a castle of crystallized cherry. She must learn to make for the Europeans a chocolate mousse with whorls of whipped cream, a fine straw-coloured consommé where prawns would swim, for the Americans mango ice-cream, not too fibrous, to give the idea of local colour at Carib's Rest. How to make croissants, éclairs, the little things for which the visitor, if he begins to miss them, will all at once decide to pack up and go home. And for the British, although there were every year fewer of them in number at St James, a Queen of Puddings as heavy and significant as the Empire at the height of its glory.

You know [Lore said in a letter about that time], I went round to Teza's house. It was raining cats and dogs. I think I'll come and join you in the glorious Tropics, Holly, if you're not careful. Ask Sanjay if he doesn't need someone to invent new cocktails in his famous Bar. Everyone's so miserable here, too.

The door was opened by a big black woman and she looked pretty sad as well. Fancy being sent over here to learn to cook! But she said Teza was kind to her and there was another friend, Ford, who had found her a room in a squat where he is in Stoke Newington. It turns out the woman who owns the posh hotel on your island didn't give Millie nearly enough to live on in London, as well as pay for the course at Cuisine Française School, which is quite near where Teza lives, as it happens. Anyway, I put two and two together and I remembered your searing account of the day you went up to the village and Teza met Ford hanging around up there, and there'd been a good, kind woman who gave Teza a bed. So that's Millie. She tells me there are smart houses now on St James with French tiles on the roof and Italian tiles on the floor and Spanish tiles, oh Lord, all over the bathroom and she started me off laughing – the first time for a month or two, I can tell you.

I asked Millie why Ford was living in this squat some way away. But she just shrugged. 'I thought Ford and Teza lived together here,' I said. Mind you I hadn't been around for longer than I thought. I don't know what it is in London: in Chelsea you just feel you're under the river all the year round and the seasons never change, and then you go up Portobello way and you find there's cherries and melons in the market and the last time there was leeks and spuds. This time it was corn on the cob, hazelnuts, blackberries, Cox's orange pippins. I'd bought a bunch of those Michaelmas daisies for Teza and a punnet of blackberries too. 'You making blackberry and apple tart at the Cuisine Française?' I asked Millie but she just shook her head and rolled her eyes like a fruit machine. 'Flan,' she said at last in a really comic voice and we rolled about again.

Then she got up and went to the door and opened it, and sure enough her ears are sharper than mine and there was someone standing out there. Just as I said, fancy that, Holly, the funniest looking little kid. So I was right – Teza had been kind of restless last time I saw her – it wasn't that she was likely to have a baby to pass the time, if you know what I mean, it was that she had one hidden away already. 'Why on earth didn't she say so before?' I said to Millie when I'd recovered from staring at the little creature. 'What's been going on here anyway?'

It turned out that Teza's aunt, her mother's sister, was pretty elderly and lived in a great house in Suffolk or somewhere and was due to leave her remaining fortune to Teza. 'Now aren't some people greedy?' I couldn't help thinking, when Teza's mother had already left her enough to buy this house off the Portobello Road and money for donations to Black Power too, I wouldn't wonder. This aunt was a strict Baptist, Millie says – and there's some respect in her voice. There's a lot of all that in the islands, I suppose, so you can see why Millie would understand what seems pretty barbaric to me, i.e. covering up the birth of your illegitimate half-caste (for that's how Teza's aunt would doubtless label the child) in order to inherit later. Now, evidently, the aunt has died and the baby can come out of the closet, as you might say. 'So Teza lives alone now, does she?' I say. And I couldn't help asking about Ford.

Obviously, Millie was thrilled that Ford had kept in touch over the years. He'd sent her cards, he told her she should come over and the Party would send a fare. There was an American Black Panther coming and there'd be a big meeting . . . and there'd be 'Onward Christian Soldiers' for Millie to sing, as well as meet a lot of new friends. But something held her back – she'd worked for people too long to do something without being told to. God, I'm getting like that myself, Holly. Just about creep into the Green Velveteen with the hangover of the century and totter round with the Green Velvet Special (new since your day, crème de menthe and coffee shaken up with crushed ice and a spot of orange bitters). I'll say, 'Yes, please' when they announce I'm to work right over the Yuletide Season without a break. Just like the way Millie waited till Mrs Van der Pyck pushed her on the *Singer* with her ticket on the LIAT plane from St Jude to Barbados in one hand and her bag and Bible in the other. She was very sick too on the flight in the Jumbo from Barbados to London because they put her in the tail of the plane and it swung around all over the place. She thought she was going to die, Millie said, like being inside the belly of a whale. And Ford was there to meet her at the airport! She was happy in the squat, except Howard and Lucy, some white couple in the rock record business, who were in the squat too, were terribly dirty. And most nights there was the sound of breaking glass.

Ford had moved out some time ago, she said. (Sorry I'm so bad on when, it must be an age since I went up Portobello Road way. You know, Holly, I rather like it round there. I think I'll move – and maybe you'll feel like coming back one day and joining me, it'll be like the old days except we're one hell of a lot older. But you must get tired of sitting on your rock sometimes, despite the weather!)

When I asked why Ford had gone, Millie just shrugged again. I daresay his interests had moved away from Teza's quite a bit by then, he was all Black Power. And also he's been taken up in a big way by the glitterati (Eng. Lits. and media and money with a touch of art) and Teza wasn't included in the invitation. That made me feel a bit sorry for her, even if she is now a rich lady living on her own. And honestly, Holly, as soon as you see Teza you remember her charm. Even though her eyebrows are all knitted up with theory and how feminism must be free of sexism before it can reach the aspired-for level of socialism, she's still somehow good to be with. She came down the stairs and caught the little kid into her arms on the landing and gave a really nice friendly laugh when she saw me. 'Hi, Lore,' she said. 'Let's have a drink and then I'll take you to a new stall in the market where they've got the most lovely textiles you ever saw. Coming?'

You remember all those pieces of fabric we used to hoard, Holly? Well Teza's not interested in that sort of thing herself, but she likes to give pleasure to others. That's how I see it – on a rainy day and all – and no doubt a million pamphlets to get out for the sisterhood or whatever in the pipeline. 'What about the baby?' I said, after making all the usual remarks that it's the most lovely little child I'd ever seen, etc. 'She'll stay with Millie,' Teza said, smiling. 'It's an Ibo fabric stall I'm going to show you. You'll be able to hang the cloth on your walls or make a tablecloth or cushions. You can make one for me while you're about it.'

It was really great seeing Teza again. I said I was thinking of moving round here myself and she said why not come and live in her basement? All this money has made her generous, and that's not how it takes most people. Millie looked happy too, and she smiled quite motherly at Teza when she handed over the little kid and we left. 'It's a pity Millie can't stay forever and help you out,' I said, because my admiration for Teza was growing with each minute. I mean there she is abandoned by her boyfriend and father of her child just when she needs support. It's all very well, money isn't everything. 'Well, yes,' Teza said, and then we were out of the house and walking down the empty, rainy market to this incredible old Nigerian who sells rugs and textiles patterned like nothing you've seen in your life before, Holly.

It's been difficult for me out here, trying to imagine the changes at home – and in America too, of course, but the kind of man and woman you get coming down from the States are definitely the unreconstructed sort. The women are covered in scarlet nail polish and the men hold the door open for them, and at night in the little converted slave cottages at the side of Carib's Rest you hear them helping themselves to ice and liquor from the fridge and sobbing and shouting at each other. The jet set's a bit more cool – there was a Princess something who had a vibrator and a pistol in her bag – but usually when they go you find nothing but syringes, they're too far out of it to leave a tip.

Maybe I look back a little too sentimentally to the old days in King's Road and West London, but it seems to me that Lore, Teza and I had just about the best time three girls – you say women now, of course, I know that – could have had at any time in history. London was doing all this swinging, and even though the tourists and the magazine editors did all they could to cash in on it, it just happened by itself, wherever it felt like happening. Lore's hair was short and curly and she looked like a sexy, grinning chestnut. Teza's long cornfield hair came down as low as the top of her mini, and the Slavonic side of her was most in evidence then. Perhaps it was before the English mother had asserted her side of the family by making over funds and all that. Teza was certainly totally broke. And I – they all said I looked a bit like Ava Gardner. It was just the time old movies were becoming a cult on their own. A couple of gays had a gigantic collection of portraits of Garbo and Dietrich and Crawford, etc., and the mags printed them large. We dressed in all colours like the Pied Piper of Hamlin by day and lay in the parks, stoned; at night we drew on Cupid's bows and went dancing in our beaded thirties gowns from the antique supermarket. Most girls, even if they did buy a poster of the dead and beautiful Che Guevara, still thought under-development was to do with your cup size in a bra.

Once I realized I was well and truly stranded here and Lore wrote me about the fashions and whatever was going on, I began to feel like Robinson Crusoe, starting out from scratch on a desert island. It seems the more women's consciousness was raised, the further the hemline went down. I had to sew about six minis together to get a skirt that came to the new length – and then after all that I felt like a suffragette who'd got washed up after a shipwreck. And the longer I stayed on here the more uncertain I became about going back at all. I'd be Rip Van Winkle by now. But it's one of the factors, I'm sure, that goes to make up my lack of understanding of the new relationships. It's not just that men nowadays seem to want to take half the responsibility for the home and the kids and so on and take courses in ante-natal breathing exercises. It's the new way of splitting apart, too. Teza really wanted Ford to feel free, as Lore told me that time she came out here and we managed to have a good talk – when the men weren't circling round Lore in the Bar, that is. (She still knows how to do it. In the end she was so hassled she had to go and spend the night with Ferdie the barman. At least he doesn't want to give me anything, she said.) Teza knew she could survive without Ford because she had learned to be a committed feminist. And the Black Panthers were making remarks like a woman's position was best under a man or something like that. No wonder it didn't appeal to Teza. At the same time, Ford did enjoy his new position as the great West Indian talent, discovered by Julian Byrne, the critic and mentor of taste, and a lovely white lady with a castle in Scotland that had a moat, and a couple of literary editors who had pull in the States as well and could make Ford's name worldwide. He had no need for a dingy-looking group of women turning up every night at the house off Portobello Road and making the place stink of take-away while they aired their grievances. He'd swagger in late and call to Teza to fix him a drink, and all hell was let loose.

So what else is new? I say to myself every time I read of a new thing like palimony – or women preaching in church – or businesswomen in America with marsupial briefcases that hold stiletto-heel shoes for putting on after the Nikes they'd jogged to the office in. I'm from a really distant past, and OK I look like a dinosaur too. But I genuinely didn't recognize Ford when he came into the store just under two months ago.

Counter, curtain of beads, stained-wood floor where the fruit squash in when it fall from the basket – big freezer like a punishment cell, holding wild meat and poor fat pre-packed turkey for the Christmas blow-out. Nothing's different since then – even the helicopter going overhead, and the humming of the generator out there by the chicken shed. The only thing that's different is that instead of Ford, smiling coolly at me in the beret and the NH glasses without rims and the eyes much too big behind them, there's this tiresome girl with her hands spread palm down on the counter top. '*Where is Ford?*' Who tells her to come here and ask me that? Who gives her permission to swim over into my private life here anyway?

'Please go in there a moment,' I say to the girl, indicating the Craft Centre. I can see Sanjay's shadow on the concrete walkway outside and hear the patter of his daughter's footsteps after him. 'You'll get in trouble,' I say to the girl – and Millie takes the opportunity to wash her hands of the whole thing and go out through the swinging conches for the last time, swaying hugely, bowed down with carrier bags. 'You didn't go through customs, did you?' I say in my most menacing voice, as it seems that to cap it all the girl has it in mind to disobey me. 'This is the proprietor of the island coming in now,' I hiss. 'He can have you taken for interrogation in Trinidad.'

'OK.' The girl moved her shoulders in a faint shrug of disdain, as if she knows as well as I do that customs formalities only take place here once a week when the *Singer* docks, and people from yachts can come and go as they please. And I see as she swings past me and down the one step to the Craft Centre that she has a slight smile on her face. The impertinence! I see too a birthmark, white, something like an unripe Alpine strawberry, on that lovely long neck under the chin. Butter wouldn't melt in *her* mouth, I think. And on she walks – and her legs part as neatly as scissors and she's gone from sight altogether. The saucy creature has climbed right into Jim Davy's priceless pre-Columbian pot! Now what the heck am I going to do? And I feel suddenly a fatigue that merges in with Sanjay's face and battered white suit with the image of Ford in his combat jacket and those sweet, kind eyes smiling out at me. Whatever people may say, Millie was right. He's a sweet boy and he stayed one. But where is he now? And how much was Sanjay to blame?

'Hello, Holly.' Sanjay came and leaned with one elbow on the counter like he always does. It's a semi-confidential but still lordly stance. He likes to stay quiet for a time before asking with a self-deprecating smile for an orangeade. But today I've no time for this type of thing. Any minute, after all, that bloody girl may break her way out of the pot and – I can't imagine what.

'Yes, you can leave it in the Craft Centre,' Sanjay said to Jim Davy when the beautiful thing was brought ashore, as exciting as finding a dolphin close-up. 'But don't forget it's beyond value.'

'What's that great urn thing, Holly?' Ford said too, when he came two months ago and he'd had to tell me who he was. And I realized he was just the same really. We kissed, as if that time with Teza all those years ago had somehow been the turning point of all our lives.

'I have poems about beautiful great pots like this, you know, Holly,' he said; and I felt embarrassed that everyone on St James had decided somehow to ignore the fame and talent of Ford – which you could understand with someone like Mrs Van der Pyck, but Sanjay reads Shakespeare and *Tom Jones* and things like that out on the verandah by his paraffin lamp. I suppose it took me a long time to figure out that Sanjay hears news from London too, and as far as he's concerned, Ford has spent years fighting for his overthrow. Yet – you have to hand it to Sanjay – he'd laugh and joke with Ford if he turned up one day, like these little differences of opinion were miles below him.

'It was found at Laughing Gull Bay,' I said to Ford, and he turned and made a shrieking noise like one of those laughing gulls that keep me awake in my room at The Heights. For Ford was always merry – I remember that evening in the Coconut Bar, after our picnic at the Lagoon and before he and Teza slipped away in the canoe. He made you laugh when you weren't expecting to. There was kindness and thought in there, too. He wasn't a frivolous person even then, not Ford.

'It's a vessel for the blood of human sacrifice,' he said then. 'An ancient Mayan ritual, Holly. That's where they came from.' And he went over and stroked the belly of the pot. I felt a bit scared. I thought of one of Lore's letters, where she described that Panther's speech where he said that if things didn't change, a lot of white blood would flow like water before we attain our rightful desires. Poor Ford – whose blood was it that spoilt the millionaire's blue water half a mile away down Union Bay?

'I'll have an orangeade,' says Sanjay, leaning a little closer on his patched elbow. 'And an ice-cream,' he adds hurriedly, for Pandora, dragging her steps like a tired child, stands crowned by the beads and shells in the curtain like she's just been pulled out of the sea.

'And how's your baby, Ford?' I said that time, and he said, 'What baby?' and we both laughed because there's a way here, where the blooms never change and the sun is always up there or right down under your feet, that you can't tell the passing of time. Yet, after he'd gone I thought maybe he meant she's a big girl now, no baby, and you're no chicken either, Holly. Or maybe he just couldn't recall walking out on Teza – on purpose by mistake he's forgotten the whole episode, so to speak. I certainly hope they don't change the laws too quickly that the man need pay no maintenance in these liberated days, before the women get right on top.

There was a snuffle from the big brown pot and Sanjay swung round. He's so relaxed in his manner, but he's as paranoid as the rest of us, you bet. Then his face smoothed out again. My heart was in my shoes but it was OK because Sanjay thought the snuffle came from his daughter Pandora and God knows the wretched girl cries enough. She's standing behind Sanjay now, with one hand on his arm and he's trying not to look irritated. It's a shame the gringos bombed the madhouse in Grenada, but it's no reason for her not to be sent off somewhere else, I say. And she came up to me and said in that little-girl voice, 'A Raspberry Ripple, please,' which is about the only ice-cream name she seems to have by heart. And I go with her to the big freezer and Sanjay comes too: thank heaven it's as far as you can get from the Craft Centre door.

'So what's new, Holly?' Sanjay says in his quiet, confidential tone, while I hand the poor girl her ice. Her face is quite red and blotchy, and it looks like she's always crying. And I knew as I said, 'Nothing's new', and Sanjay pretended to look in his trousers for change, and I said 'I'll mark it up', that there *was* something new – and bad news too, and not so far from where we were standing. For when Sanjay and Pandora had taken their interminable time leaving, with Pandora dropping her ice and trying to scoop it up and Sanjay talking to her with love and exasperation, like you do to a child at the end of a long, long day, I went quietly into the Craft Centre and peered down into the neck of the pot. The girl looked up at me, bold as brass.

'You're Holly, I know,' she said. 'And you were a friend of my mother, Teza. Ford is my father, see?'

EVENING

Evening in the tropics – the time the white man of Empire traditionally sat down with a sundowner, or a sun's-over-the-yardarm, or a noggin brought in by silent servants – came to Carib's Rest Hotel, with its usual violet hush. A persimmon sky leaked over the verandah, where a white man did indeed sit, a copy of the London *Times* unfolded on his lap. His lip, upper and stiff. Dark hair so flattened down and made brilliant it looked ready to reflect the stars. Yet somewhere, in the small, hard eyes that had seen Eton and Christchurch and Teheran and Vientiane, Laos, and the starving crowds of Ethiopia, was a shifty, amused look. Although there were rumours that this man so obviously fitting the requirements must be a spy, it was also argued that it is hard to tell where sensitive reporting ends and espionage begins. Things did mysteriously happen when Maldwin Carr had just left a place – or they happened just before he turned up. But then he could claim that that was why in the first place he was there.

The yacht lying out at anchor on a placid sea had been chartered in Barbados by Maldwin Carr. He was a first-class sailor and had taken only one crew on board – apart from the girl, of course, who was cook. More trouble was expected in this corner of the eastern Caribbean. Why else, as they gossiped in the London clubs where in December great flares were lit, showing a Christmas-cakey St James's Palace through the rain or sudden gusts of hard, white hail, would Lockton, proprietor of the famous newspaper that employs Mal Carr, send him out there? And why was he, Mal Carr, the recipient of so enormous a salary? (Not that anyone knows what it is, but the amount in gossip currency rises and falls at lunch and dinner in the club, depending on whether it's a bull or bear market.)

The answer, so it goes, is this. Mal Carr has such impeccable credentials, such agate integrity, that readers of this famous paper would no more think of mistrusting his judgement as the result of his investigations than they would think of performing a citizen's arrest on Alec Guinness as Smiley or Sean Connery as Bond. Everyone knows that Maldwin Carr has his shirts made to measure at Turnbull and Asser and his Stilton to send to Lady Anthea at Christmas from Paxton and Whitfield, both in Jermyn Street, of course. So much the better. In this Royal Park of England, dreams take a long time to die. So even if Lockton has interests in Latin America and an obvious interest in preventing a left-wing régime from taking hold in islands adjacent to Grenada, his dispatching of Maldwin Carr to look at the situation in depth is entirely balanced and fair. Carr's articles will be read with the port and cigars at the clubs in St James's, and in humbler homes, in garden cities and shires. And many of the readers will do no more than reflect with relief on how wise they were not to have booked a 'luxury holiday' in the Caribbean after all.

An hour earlier, before afternoon had gone over into evening, Maldwin Carr stood on the verandah of Carib's Rest and watched a strange dance, or so it seemed, take place round a ramshackle building by the scuffed track that runs parallel to the beach. He had his bearings by now – the lagoon with, above it, the old wooden house that had belonged to the cadet branch of the Allard family in the south; a flat stretch above the lagoon as far as the Coconut Bar, where yachts moored; above that the northern end of the island, where the consortium had built houses for winter visitors and sprinklers turned like dancers in a water ballet, forcing the coarse grass green. Above that, the remains of old Allard's house – but for some reason the consortium hadn't wanted it and after sixteen years it is almost a ruin. And on the windward side of St James, where the great rollers come in and the sand is white as icing sugar, Man o' War Beach and Laughing Gull Bay. Carr could see the village if he strolled to the southern part of the verandah that stretches round the first floor of the hotel, once the cottonhouse. And he did so, passing the hotel macaws in a cage and pulling a frangipani blossom that had strayed into the passageway and sticking it in his buttonhole.

Mrs Van der Pyck walked from the long principal room and joined the new visitor. He had requested a sea-view room and she had given him the best, looking straight out to sea over the store and on the right the Bar with its picturesque thatched hat. Now the visitor was asking for another vodka and some of that excellent fresh ginger beer and Mrs Van der Pyck was simpering and waving to the barman, who stood by the bar at the end of the panelled room.

'It seems there's one part of the island that can't be seen from here,' Maldwin Carr said. His tone he invariably kept dry and self-deprecating, as if he were the fool and would join quietly in the laughter when his foolishness was shown up.

'No need to see that!' said Mrs Van der Pyck, as she stood at what might be imagined to be an elegant angle to the verandah rail. With her dark, hennaed hair and white chiffon pleated dress she could have been an illustration – there were enough romances set in these parts, God knows – on the cover of a book of a beautiful woman and a distinguished man meeting somewhere in the equatorial islands and falling in love. But women were often quickly aware of Maldwin Carr's sexual ambiguity; and Mrs Van der Pyck kept her distance still.

'It's an absolute slum,' she said. She couldn't think why Sanjay hadn't had The Heights cleared years ago, when he came into the land. After all, it was in the southern part of the island. But then, why did old Mr Allard make such a strange will? Why should Sanjay have only seventeen years or so? Of course, she knew the answer. Old Allard got a better price from the consortium if a shortish lease was attached to the southern half. At the same time, the island could remain to all intents and purposes British. He had seen independence coming, which would mean increased dependence on America. He was a clever old brute, everyone said so who'd known him here.

No, she hadn't been on St James when the old man was alive, Mrs Van der Pyck said, as Maldwin Carr drifted just a foot or two away from her and took up a position by the opening to the elegant long room. She'd come to St James shortly after . . . It had been a terrible business clearing this place up and getting it going, as he must probably see. But it was worth it. They'd had the Vice-President's mother down here with a party only last month. So, yes, confidence in these parts was returning. Well, look at the welcome the Americans had been given in Grenada. And she did pride herself on the best food for nautical miles around. It was nice too to meet an Englishman who had the time and money to charter a yacht and while away the sunny hours round the islands . . . How she wished she had some of that time, though she could always get away for a couple of days, for there was such a trustworthy staff. . .

Maldwin Carr, who had by this time turned 180 degrees on his heel, had looked over the rail down towards the beach. He'd seen a man in a battered white suit make his way into the store. A girl of about eighteen ran in after him – but at first, like a child, she'd hung around on the concrete walk-way. Now Maldwin saw the exodus of the man in the white suit and a woman – this time – at his side, in a floral dress. Maldwin pointed down and asked Mrs Van der Pyck who this woman could be.

'Holly Baker,' Mrs Van der Pyck spat out the name. 'Now *she* lives in The Heights. Yes, there's an example for you. I really wouldn't go near the place!'

Maldwin Carr, veteran of street fighting in Beirut, massacre in Kampuchea and Kampala, as well as of thoughtful poetic treks in search of the marsh Arab or southern Afghan nomad, seemed unalarmed by this. 'The gentleman must, of course, be Mr Allard,' he said.

'You'll meet him later! He always comes to Christmas dinner here!' Mrs Van der Pyck's voice retained its sharpness. And she went on: 'Sanjay's poor daughter, bombed out of the Grenada madhouse, looked after by a local woman down at the Allard house on the lagoon . . . and his wife died of . . .' but Mrs Van der Pyck's voice was now trailing away. For the dance continued unexpectedly at the foot of her carefully mown and bougainvillea-planted lawn. A girl had now come out of the store. The girl was slim and bronzish in colour and she stood staring at Mr James Allard and his poor cracked daughter as they made their way back down the beach to the lagoon. Who can *she* be? it was Mrs Van der Pyck's turn to wonder, and then to wonder again when the impeccable Englishman said that the girl, for the duration of the cruise, was his cook. She'd come out with him on his yacht. And she was coming up the hill at his invitation to join him for a drink.

'Ford is dead,' I said to the girl. Except I didn't. I watched her climb out of that great brown jar with the swirls of paint thousands of years old and I thought, as she walked to the door and looked after Sanjay and his daughter, she's a figure who could have walked from a Greek vase, a terracotta figure with slim waist and hips and breasts like a boy's. There's no break in the ocean as it goes round the earth from the Mediterranean to the Caribbean Sea after all.

But I said instead, 'Who's that man up there at the hotel? He's off the yacht, isn't he?' and I stared up, irritated at the way he leaned so nonchalantly on the balustrade of the verandah, with Mrs Van der Pyck ogling at his side.

'I cook for him,' the girl said. Then she pointed down the beach at the retreating figure of Sanjay. 'He's to blame,' she said. 'He killed my father, didn't he?'

I don't know how you get out of these things. The girl had come back to the counter and was looking me straight in the eye.

'You're Mari,' I said. 'Lore told me about you. You're making a mistake. Go home.'

Lore wrote me after she got back from her visit out here, that things were getting quite out of hand in London now. She'd moved into Teza's – and already she could hardly believe she'd been here, those brief two days when she came over on the *Singer* and left again on one of the yachts. (It's so easy, she can just sit in the Coconut Bar and she'll get offered a cruise all round the world. But I like to go on my own. When I go, when my Colt .22 comes from the States, it'll be at the helm of my own motor cruiser.)

When Lore came, she had already moved into the basement of Teza's house and she said Teza's daughter was hanging around asking too many questions, making trouble.

'It's quite nice here,' Lore said. 'But I'm beginning to see why Teza said I could stay for no rent, just pay the electricity. Teza's daughter – Mari – she's developed an obsession about Ford. I'm supposed to remember everything I can about him. But it's so hazy. Mari ought to be sent away to school or something. God knows, Teza has money enough. But I knew this would happen to me, Holly. I'm the surrogate mother while Teza camps out on Greenham Common. Mari's a nice girl. A sharp London girl. You know. But she ought to be got away from this mania about her father, it just isn't healthy at all.'

Roots, roots, roots, I thought, as I read Lore's letter, when she said there was lots of people coming round to the house now and Mari was excited, she imagined she was on the trail. That's all people want nowadays. You can even find out who your real parents are if you've been adopted, these days, when you're eighteen. And Mari must be about sixteen I suppose – no wonder she's desperate to find out what she can. For Teza had done that incredibly stupid thing, she'd refused to talk about Ford with Mari at all.

'It's not that Mari feels particularly keenly towards Teza,' Lore said as we sat sipping our rum punches, waiting for the rain – for Lore came in off-peak season, it's cheaper then. (It's a time of waiting – for a hurricane, for rain and the stink of fresh greenery before it all rots in the sun at midday.) Teza was a bit – well, brisk with the girl, it seems. She was militantly independent – so Mari must be too. 'There weren't many men to be seen in that house near the Portobello Road,' Lore said with a laugh. She had to ask any man who came to visit her to creep down the basement quiet-like, if it was late at night. Teza never said anything if she came down and saw you with a bloke in the mornings, but you felt uneasy, like it was time to move out and go somewhere else. Mari, for a fact, had been sent up to the clinic for the Pill when she was fourteen, but Lore could have sworn blind she'd never had it off with a soul. It was too much of a responsibility, somehow, with Teza standing there in the background preparing to be a single grandparent and indoctrinate the child with her beliefs. Moreover, it would be born despite the Pill (for Teza didn't believe there was such a thing as real protection against Nature's intentions, vile always as far as women are concerned). Maybe she's right too, I think sometimes when I look at the lives we've all led. But to hell with it. Whose is better, anyway? Who would have wanted to be Duchess

Dora, with all the money in the world and plenty of time to read the books Sanjay brought out that rotted with damp in the old library down by the lagoon?

'The trouble was that Mari wanted me to come with her on the quest for her father – and I had to help her,' Lore said, 'with Teza away and risking arrest daily. Where does what-you-do-for-your-flesh-and-blood and what-you-do-for-the-world begin? I've had to ask myself.'

'I wonder that too,' I said, and Ferdie brought us more of the gold rum and mango and papaya juices and a sweet peppering of fresh nutmeg from the tree. 'That's what we've always wanted to know,' I said. 'At least Teza is trying to stop us all being blown up by the bomb.'

'While her daughter suffers alone,' Lore said.

And now here's Mari, ready to blow up the whole world by the looks of her, that's the irony of it all.

It was a question at first, apparently, of Mari finding a photo of Ford in the writing desk of the sitting room that Teza did up, surprisingly good-taste and stripped-pine for a woman of such revolutionary and uncompromising views. She found it in the old rosewood desk, against a wall stippled pale orange – on a floor of polished boards with the odd kelim dotted here and there (Lore said it was agony when Teza had meetings, with the thumping on the floor above). It was classic really, Lore said. Finding a photo in a drawer. Nineteenth-century style. Until she saw it there and a ring with a little locket built in and another tiny photo inside that, with a lock of Teza's hair round it – until then, she said, she hadn't been sure whether Ford was her father or not. After all, Teza hardly liked to acknowledge fatherhood in the new matriarchy. But she had been in love with him once, she must have been. It was tragic, Lore said, that Mari came down to the basement holding the ring and the photo as if she'd just stumbled on the answer to the riddle of the Sphinx, or something: 'Wasn't Teza's hair *yellow* then?' And so on. The poor girl was crying . . . and Mari was a tough London girl, she'd say it again, it was really pitiful to see.

Lore is a good sort, really. She may say she had no choice but to help Mari look for her father, but there's not many that wouldn't have just packed their bags and left. I mean, it's a heavy assignment. And when Ford *was* finally confronted with his daughter, who's to say he'd be welcoming? Lore did it out of the kindness of her heart. And I hope I find the kindness myself not to blurt anything out to the girl in the short time she's here. Because she sure has to go soon.

I knew bad news when I saw that spider-girl swimming over in the glare of the sun, at that hour in the afternoon where everything goes double, and the girl swam above her spider shadow to bring us all more trouble here.

How can I say that Ford walked into this store just a few weeks ago and denied his own daughter – or as good as, anyway? 'You might say that it's lucky,' I tell Lore in my thoughts – for I need Lore now. Lucky that Ford left here before Mari could discover the truth. Which is that all her efforts to find her father would have gone unrewarded anyway.

'. . . the man they call Sanjay.' The girl is standing by the counter and then she has to step back because one of those yachting-cap-and-shorts-with-legs-like-German-sausage comes in – I can't even remember his name, he's from the villa with the oleanders and the keskidees caged up out the back.

'Well, Holly,' he says. 'And how's my lady pirate, wanderer of the seven seas today?' He glances sideways at Mari, his interest immediately disguised by an apparent keenness on the display of suntan lotion – Ambre Solaire, a coconut oil to burn the white people till they go blotched as poor Pandora, Johnson's Baby Oil for the millionaire women who like to say they keep their beauty preparations to a minimum. 'Guess I'll have one of these,' he mutters. Grey and pink, like a skinned armadillo he stands next to tawny Mari; and she feels his eye on her crotch and moves out to the concrete walkway outside the store.

'Mari!' I cry, as the hundreds of beads and tiny molluscs tinkle behind her. 'Wait!'

But, as in a corny nightmare, it is too late. I take old yachting cap's EC dollars with fury, while he squeezes my hand as a substitute for the girl. By the time I've rung up the cash register and pulled change from the scoured drawer, the girl has gone. Striding the low hedge of hibiscus as if there were no such thing as demarcations between private and public property, a hotel lawn where the rich and white may walk and others can't (although you wouldn't find any notices saying so). I'm inured by now, I suppose, to our tiny, pettily obsessive social system. And something equally pettily ridiculous in me is shocked that the stranger Mari doesn't know you can't just walk up to Carib's Rest by crossing the hedge that divides it from Holly's store.

If such things were possible, then Holly herself might do it from time to time. Jim Davy is the only one who takes little Holly for a drink on that verandah, with its lean-back, comfortable chairs in chintzes imported by Duchess Dora from Harrods. Disregarding Mrs Van der Pyck's stony stare, Jim orders a Scorpion – a white dry-snow-cauldron of rum and eggwhite and bitter-fresh lime. We have straws to sip it with and a gardenia floats in the middle. 'Almost as good as Trader Vic's in the Hilton in London,' Lore said laughing when Jim Davy treated us both up there, and he ordered three in succession for us, as I remember. Jim Davy was asking Lore so many questions. How long had she lived in her friend Teza's house? How about the great scandal of the

Ford–Teza elopement here that Holly had told him about over and over: the meeting in the village, the picnic at the lagoon, the long hours in the dusk and the night, with the fireflies lighting up the shore from where you sit out on the raft on stilts at the far end of the Coconut Bar. Did Lore see Ford in London now? Does Ford come round and see Teza . . . and isn't there a little kid? So he's heard anyway. A romantic story, really – and Jim Davy calls for more salted peanuts to aggravate the thirst. Lore got quite drunk, I know that. But don't ask me what she said to him. Sometimes it feels like a relief, Jim Davy being off the island. 'Marry me, Holly,' he'll say when we're down in the bar and the jukebox plays 'Autumn Leaves'. 'I can give you a great life in Kansas.'

A legendary tale, the Ford–Teza story by now, it's true. No doubt because Ford became a famous poet – and involved in the black struggle too – and then disappeared off the face of the earth. It's all too late now. But even so I see this girl coming to wreck the whole scene, to cut simple pieces out of a complicated puzzle and, by jamming them together, break everything up.

So it's Sanjay the wretched girl wants. To kill him no doubt, to force him to say if Ford is dead or alive. It's Sanjay, poor Sanjay. I can smell the damp, woody smell of his shirt that day after the picnic at the lagoon when we walked back, tired, along the curve of the yellow beach to the house. Duchess Dora was tired too and she had gone to lie down. I followed Sanjay, skirting the verandah and the ropes of flowering clematis that hang down like Rapunzel's hair over the balcony. We were shaded from sight. I watched his back as he went off to the far side of the lagoon. He pushed his way through trees into the creek again – I followed – this time on the far side and in thicker jungle than ever. How can they dare come and hack it down? Put an airport there? The jungle, the twisting ropes of liana and the big butterflies that go so slowly they're like handkerchiefs raised and lowered in the streaming green – the world has found more and more ways of eroding and destroying places like this.

Sanjay had a house there. It was a sort of floor of spars and beams from an old ship that had been wrecked off the coast of St James, and there were natural curtains of hanging branches of tamarind tree and a window where you could look out between the leaves and see the creek, and opposite, in the still water, his child-size pier and the boat he'd made, riding at anchor. God knows what happened to that magical place all this time. The creek grew over entirely, I suppose, when little Pandora began to show signs of her illness and they didn't go down to play boats any more. The jungle closed in over Sanjay's forest shelter too. I don't like to go down to the lagoon now and see the scar the tractor made into a hill of red mud, and trees dying that have leaned against each other and died and come up again for thousands of years.

Sanjay and I made love on a bed of palm fronds on the floor of his house. I thought at first, what if the little girl runs in and sees us – but the jungle was too thick here for that to worry me for long. And Millie would have taken her in for her rest. Sanjay was quiet and sad and I cried when we'd finished because I felt the end of something and not the beginning, and there was something very bitter in that.

Sanjay rubbed my eyelids with his finger and smiled.

'Where were you when I was younger?' he said. And I hardly hesitated at all. I said, 'Dora . . .'

Some men make the fact of their marriage like an inadmissible secret, which if ever spoken, would bring ruin and disaster to whoever heard it. It's as if a congenital illness, a joint one, held the couple in its thrall. If at first I put Sanjay in this category it was because I sensed a weakness in him, a fierceness that had to be too strongly held down, a need for a reason for his strange life out here. Later I came to know better. I understood the shadow under which Sanjay lived, and I saw his escape into childish things – the making of miniature ships, the painstaking building of an artificial harbour, with stones and branches dragged along the jungle track – as his way of shutting out pain. And, too, he did try to love his daughter, Pandora. It was touching. When they used to come along to the Coconut Bar – when I was working there before the store was ready and Mrs Van der Pyck was issuing her fancy orders from above – Sanjay and the little girl would perch on stools, and Sanjay would wear this particularly shy smile, and the child would ask for a lime juice or a slice of water melon (we still didn't have a freezer in those days).

'You'll grow up to help Holly in the bar, Dora,' Sanjay said. 'We'll have ice-cream then, you'll see.'

'Ice-cream,' the child said, because of course she'd never had one. And Sanjay would look me in the eyes and laugh. Then he'd grow melancholy again. All very sentimental, I'm sure – but I used to wait for the moment when Millie would appear along the beach or down the track from the village, usually with a bunch of other kids in tow, and swoop little Pandora up. Then Sanjay stayed on a while. He never drank much – maybe he'd just have fresh ginger and some soda to top it up. He never said much either. But he'd look pleased if you said the new houses were coming along very well, or there had been some interesting passengers on the *Singer*, keen to meet up with the manager of the consortium's estate and buy, maybe, a plot of land for building a house. He was so cut off, poor Sanjay. As if old Allard had purposely condemned him to live out his lease in the tail end of the nineteenth century, while the new age thundered ahead in the north.

Dora. If I was asked what the shadow was which Sanjay lived all his time in fear of – when she was alive, of course, and then after that he was even more afraid – I'd make a fool of myself by saying it was the fear of her death. But that was the fact of the matter. Duchess Dora, with all her affectations and the clothes and the flowers that had to be exactly right, not vulgar, in the tropics where flowers do so terribly easily tend to be vulgar, was as delicate herself as a crocus on the equator. If it wasn't one thing, it was another. There was skin cancer – or the fear of it. And the symptoms were duly produced. There was pernicious anaemia and diabetes and hyperglucose and colitis and a womb upside down and, by the sound of it, about to fall out after the perilous experience of giving birth to Pandora. No one could count how many times a wireless signal went out to the *Singer*. Once there was even a helicopter, which landed up by the village on the flat patch where they play cricket – when there's enough kids for two teams, that is. I think the helicopter time was the time of the womb – but I can't stand the sound of the blades, as I've said, and it may all be connected with blood in my mind: blood in the sea when Ford was shot down, blood in the old bedstead in the wooden house by the lagoon; and Sanjay frightened stiff.

It was all his fault, that was the point. In London he had been a successful entrepreneur, but his ideas had suited the sixties, and when the more austere years came, his ideas were redundant, too imaginative. Maybe he was tired of money – he'd bought fine things and maybe he'd had enough of them. And the calf-bound books from great European libraries, bid for at Sotheby's, went unread anyway, except by Sanjay himself, who would creep down to the old building where the rafters disastrously leaked and pull out a handful – Shakespeare, Petronius, Ovid – I've seen him at the Bar, with a disintegrating book in his hand and a strong smell coming off it, paper mulching back in the tropics to root and tree. (Why didn't he keep the books in the house? Dora said they made her ill. She couldn't breathe when they were there.)

All his fault. Dora blamed Sanjay for staying on in St

James. When they first came out, a couple of years or so before Teza and I turned up that fateful day (for us, at least!), he'd promised his wife they were out there for a long winter holiday, that was all. How much did he care about the fall in the value of his shares on the stock exchange – from neglect and lack of supervision? How strong was the pull of the island where his family had lived in feudal grandeur before he was born?

'Living here is like lying down in your own grave,' Sanjay said to me that afternoon all those years ago. 'But I can't get up. Why? What should I get up for, I'd like to know?'

What, indeed? It was like a death dance, between two insects perhaps, the kind of thing you see pictures of in the geographic magazines.

Sanjay wouldn't leave the island; and it rewarded him by becoming all he had – everything else fell away. His staying there made Dora continually, terminally ill. So he couldn't leave her either. She'd threatened the final, vengeful method if he did, of course. Millie used to tell me she heard the suicide speeches from the verandah while she was putting Pandora to bed. (Maybe the child heard them too. Certainly her childhood with Dora must have been a hard one, before she succumbed to the madness that got her taken away – in the *Singer* again, but this time with Tanty Grace – to the asylum in Grenada.)

Then that as well was Sanjay's fault. If it hadn't been for the malodorous, unhealthy air, air where the simplest infection grew a puffy bloom overnight and antibiotics fought against impossible odds – and so on and on. Dora refused to accept that her daughter's madness was anything but physical. She'd read of the deranging effects of jellyfish bites. Wasn't Man o' War Beach called just that because it was famous for these vicious bags of transparent membrane, floating on waves too boisterous to allow for visibility? Hadn't Millie taken the child there, just a week or so before she started to see things in corners of her room and scream the house down in a voice that sounded like one possessed? Or those big tarantula spiders? Or the scorpions? All the fears of the islands came out as Dora raved and wept and dosed herself with anti-depressants, tranquillizers, vitamins. And Sanjay sat there silently, it was his fault.

'Well, Holly,' Lore wrote in answer to one of my letters when I said I was sorry for Sanjay, sorry for his life – and for mine too, for I was stuck on the island too – 'mind you, it looks to me as if it's his fault, all right. Why should a man think he can shut a woman up on a lump of earth in the middle of the sea and just expect her to live her life out with him? It's OK for him, no doubt. He's got land. He can make plans. Treat someone like wallpaper and they peel off on you.'

Maybe Lore was right. I wouldn't have liked to ask Teza what she thought of it all. Because Teza, with her abstract love of women, her pure vision of equality and independence and sisterhood and freedom, couldn't stand the sight of Dora from the first. 'But Teza!' I said even then. For her dislike was so great it seemed irrational. (Those days on the island when I thought I'd be leaving too, with Teza, I'd felt nothing much either way about Dora, except to say her name to Sanjay that afternoon in the house of leaves in the lagoon – Dora. To show his remark was pointless. Where had *he* been when he was younger, for that matter? With Dora, was the answer, he had a wife.) But Teza had shrugged off my timid suggestion that Dora was a woman after all, there was no need to hate her with such vehemence.

'You have no idea what you're talking about,' Teza said. Her eyes were very open, candid-looking, a way she had when she was impatient and annoyed. 'She's a traitor. Worse than being a class traitor, a traitor to her sex. The chief enemy. The symbol of feminine weakness.' And Teza turned on her heel and walked away.

But I can't help feeling sorry for them both. Dora because she was trapped in a dream that didn't even belong to her husband but to his dead family – a pretty horrible dream too, when you come to think of it: slaves, cotton, sugar, idleness, frippery. And Sanjay was trapped in his fault. It was all his fault. And now the girl comes here – and she says it again, straight off. 'Sanjay. Sanjay is to blame.' Who told her that? How can I tell if I might think so too?

Maldwin Carr had come a long way in order to arrive at this precise moment: sunset on Christmas Eve on an island where the outline of Grenada, one of a chain of sad, thickly green islands in the blue, stood bottomless and roofless in the evening mist. He replaced his binoculars in their case and turned to smile at the girl who had climbed the hill from the store to join him for a drink. Aloft, blouse billowing in dudgeon, Mrs Van der Pyck took the order for two Stinger Sundowners into the barman in the long, panelled room. Her instinct for once had been wrong. Mr Carr was not homosexual. He had a beautiful and nubile girl as his companion for the evening's festivities. Mrs Van der Pyck was growing old, would soon be sexless as an old woman in a park feeding ducks. She instructed the barman that a generous amount of angostura bitters should be added to the already potent cocktail, which was an invention of her late South African husband. Vodka went in, Cointreau, Cinzano Rosé, lemon twist, the bitters making a pink-gin effect that matched the glare of the evening light on the verandah. Mr Carr and his girl should enjoy their Christmas celebration in St James.

It had meant a series of island-hoppings to find the girl and bring her out here. First, the island of Maldwin Carr's London: the clubs, the Savoy Grill where he lunched with Lockton and was asked to investigate a possible landing on the island of St James from Grenada by the extreme left

Revolutionary Party, the 'Pol Pot régime of the Caribbean', as Fidel Castro had described them.

The leader of the Revolutionaries, Hudson Austin, was in jail in Grenada with his accomplices after the failed coup and the American invasion, but there were rumours that remaining members of the party had taken to the hills of Grenada and were planning to infiltrate St James and use it as a base for their violent brand of Marxism-Leninism. Lockton had many interests in Venezuela and El Salvador. There was no interest for him at all in seeing a toy resort island in the middle of the trade route through the Grenadines become a trading post instead for Russian warheads and increased political instability. Two problems here, the newspaper proprietor confided. One was the ex-Black Power leader and internationally acclaimed poet, Ford, who had been missing since the end of October. Why had inquiries into the poet's whereabouts, after his failure to collect the American Endeavor Prize (awarded to black writers who had done most to bring harmony to an explosive interracial situation anywhere in the world), come up with nothing at all? Had Ford perhaps gone back to his home, St James, in the Caribbean, to foment revolution? You could never tell with these fellows. They changed their position every two minutes, funny thing.

Lockton said that rumours had come to him that a landing from Grenada by the Hudson Austin faction had indeed been planned on St James in late October. It was foiled. And Ford the poet had not been heard of since.

The second problem was that the island was still part-owned by an eccentric chap, James Allard by name. His lease would run out in the New Year, but apparently the land in the south of the island was in parts virtually impenetrable jungle. Perfect for a concealed landing from the south, no doubt. He still had the power to forbid trespassers on his land – but for some reason he'd permitted the American–Venezuelan consortium who'd bought the north end of the island from his uncle to start flattening a part of the wooded area for the building of an airport. Most winter visitors in St James were based in Caracas. They already had a private airport in the centre of that city in case of urgent need for an escape route in times of social unrest. Now, rather than have to go via Trinidad, they wanted to be able to fly their planes in to St James directly. Also, of course, the airport would be useful for flying up to the United States on business matters.

'Allard,' Maldwin Carr said in his gentle, ruminative voice. He'd been at school with James Allard. 'Not such a bad family, at least one of them,' he said. In 1876, in the Federation Riots fanned by Pope-Hennessy in Barbados and spreading like wildfire to the Windwards, the Allard of the day had greeted the maverick Governor with open arms and feasted him at his home while handing out free provisions to his own labourers in St James. For, Pope-Hennessy, horrified by the conditions he had found on his appointment as Governor to Barbados – starvation, floggings of an unbelievable severity in the prisons – had decided, after his pleas for a more lenient attitude had been scorned by indigenous landowners and British Parliament alike, to stir up trouble in the islands among the blacks and to turn a blind eye when crops and property were raided. None of this made the Governor popular, of course, and he was soon sent home.

'But,' said Maldwin with that unassuming voice suggesting a liberal outlook that too brash a commercial personage would be foolish to overlook, 'old Allard of those days was a splendid fellow. Apparently he even laid on a dance as well as a banquet for the workers, with sucking-pig on a spit and as much rum as anyone could drink, and they all revelled together till dawn.'

'Very nice,' said Lockton, drily.

'And James Allard – the one who's out there now – isn't such a bad sort either. Allard – they call him Sanjay – has a museum of oddities. Like those famous eccentrics in the eighteenth century: Don Saltero, for instance, who collected all manner of impossible things. Allard's even had a plaster copy made of the famous Slave making love to his Mistress – their petrified bodies of course, caught in the flow of the lava from Vesuvius. From Pompeii.'

'Extraordinary,' Lockton said in a cool tone.

'Sanjay Allard is a kind man,' Carr said, 'an old-fashioned liberal, you might say – and, funnily enough, there probably isn't all that much difference between him and the late, lamented Maurice Bishop, the saviour of Grenada, who was feared and loathed by the Americans and the fanatical left alike. Both men with the same aim, depending on how you look at it. A fair deal, a sense of identity for the islanders. In Sanjay's case he is just too bloody naive. The consortium isn't going to give the inhabitants a welfare state, you bet. With Bishop – well, he was indecisive. He let his deputy, Coard, walk all over him. Sad thing, really.'

'And Mr Sanjay will let Mr Hudson Austin and Mr Coard's men walk all over St James?' asked Lockton. 'That's what I want you to go and find out, Carr. After all, with an airport under construction on the island, St James could make a very useful landing point for Cuba. And if you do find a probability of insurrection, would it not be our duty to inform Her Majesty the Queen?'

'To send troops to protect the little island?' Maldwin said and laughed. The thought of toy soldiers lined up in front of Sanjay's decadent museum was somehow irresistibly comical. He said he didn't think there was a question of sending troops. 'St James is independent now. After all, no ships went out to Grenada. America is so comfortably near.'

Lockton said, 'But there's been little news of the progress of the airport recently.'

'The last I heard of the airport,' Maldwin said, 'was a joke that Sanjay was letting loose his famous collection of tropical birds there. "So *that*'s what the airport is for!" he said. His time's running out, you see,' Maldwin added, as he saw that the joke had been lost on his employer. 'So he's letting everything he owns run down – and run free.'

'And where does he expect the birds to fly to?' asked Lockton with a puzzled frown. 'The United States? Or Grenada?'

Maldwin Carr's next island involved travelling a few miles to the west. It lies between Notting Dale, the leafy, police-haunted region at the foot of Notting Hill, and Clarendon Cross, where windows of fine Bokharas face tiny shops selling cabbage and potatoes already sprouting a quiff of purplish tuber, and Golborne Road, beyond the Portobello street market's surge under the great bridge of the motorway, where trays of plastic rings and fall-apart shoes are overlooked by white giants in chintz suits and young blacks who have never seen the Caribbean. To this area, roughly the size of St James, to a dilapidated flat in a redbrick Edwardian building at the end of one of these gracious, renovated crescents, Maldwin Carr went next on his quest.

He knew that the critic and literary mentor, Julian Byrne, could be found at any time in his flat on the first floor of this building. And he inhaled with slight distaste as he went into the lobby, recognizing the faint smell of century-old economies taken from the pages of *Mrs Beeton's Household Management*. All London's Edwardian life is here – untouched, thought Maldwin Carr, suppressing a smile as the door on the first floor opened and Byrne looked out.

Julian Byrne was tall, thin to the point of ghostliness, with large, deep-brown eyes encircled by black shadows and abundant white hair. His expression was mild and vague. It would have seemed unlikely to anyone other than Maldwin that such a man should be sought out for clues in the possibly politically motivated disappearance of an Afro-Caribbean poet. And if Maldwin did not keep his ears always to the ground, detecting the subterranean crack of one social grouping as it merges with another, the unlikely juxtapositions that form and then melt away, Julian Byrne would indeed be the last person to be visited by an investigative journalist. Surely, he lives in the past, from the endless re-reading of novels of fierce restraint by Yorkshire parsons' daughters (not nearly as good as Jane Eyre, obviously) to the viewing and reviewing of stilted, permed performances by unknown actresses, old ladies now or dead. The journalist hadn't come to discuss the missing Ford's career as a poet either. He knew that Julian Byrne, with his laser eye for what is 'good' and what is 'bad', finds Ford's work – with its attempt to establish a common strand running between the Mayan and pre-Columbian societies of the South American continent, to whose neighbouring islands his ancestors were transported as slaves, and Africa, the land of beginning – merely 'self-conscious'. The fact that Ford is acclaimed worldwide is another mark against him, a guarantee of mediocrity. No: what Maldwin Carr had heard, from a girl who knows a young man who visits Julian Byrne fairly often, was that for some time the chief interest in the life of this modest and reluctant 'character' had been – in reaction perhaps against the embalmed quality of his previous interests – a strong sympathy with left-wing revolutionary politics.

'I think she's rather *frightening*,' Julian Byrne said. He gave a little giggle. 'But do go and see her. She's rather fascinating, really. Something a bit Baader-Meinhof – probably because her mother had money and rescued her Czech husband when he was working as a lavatory attendant at the Open Air Theatre, although he'd been a famous scientist in Czechoslovakia before he escaped – you know the sort of thing.'

Julian Byrne paused for breath, and Maldwin Carr, seated on a tattered ottoman, shot a quick glance at him. The description he'd been given was too vague, he thought, or perhaps this was because his informant was young and barely educated. Julian Byrne was a caricature by Beerbohm – in his black shirt and white trousers, and with the wave-crest of white hair over the eyes that seemed to have become permanently embedded in a smudge of black shadow, Maldwin Carr saw him framed on the cover of the *Yellow Book*, stooping, half-joking, arms outstreched. 'So you don't know . . . er . . . Teza particularly well?' Maldwin tried. 'I mean . . .'

'I've met her,' Julian Byrne countered. He bestowed on Maldwin Carr one of his well-known flashes of contempt. 'I simply said she was rather frightening. That's all.'

Maldwin Carr nodded in deference. The school he and Julian Byrne – ten years apart, it was true – had both been to, along with James Allard and almost everyone you could think of apart from Lockton, made the deferential nod an instant code: you could be gay as you like or live in the shires with a wife and six daughters, but women were a race apart – and faintly disgusting – all the same. 'What a marvellous photograph of Ruby Keeler,' Maldwin Carr said, to confirm and end the transmission.

Julian Byrne waved his long fingers, each one of which looked like a cigarette holder in a Shaw play, and said of the framed print of Busby Berkeley's favourite dancer over the chimneypiece, 'Yes. Isn't it *marvellous*?'

Maldwin Carr hadn't found it easy, in his quest for Ford, to draw satisfactory answers from cunning old Byrne. Inquiries as to whether the poet was known to be in England or to have gone abroad elicited: 'I *liked* his early poems, you know. I *discovered* Ford. He was so unpretentious. The poems were awfully good and funny, you know. Then – well, he allowed himself to be turned into a sort of pundit. He really became rather *embarrassing*. To tell the truth, I've no idea where he is now. Everything's perfectly all right, of course – I mean we didn't *quarrel* or anything – but I simply haven't seen him for ages.'

I wonder, Maldwin Carr thought. 'Didn't he have a

daughter?' he said. 'I remember reading a couple of months ago, when the Grenada affair blew up and everyone started looking for Ford, that a daughter was mentioned in the press. Do you know where I could contact her?'.

'Oh, I wish you *would*!' For the first time in the afternoon, Julian Byrne leaned right forward in his ancient armchair. 'She's terribly unhappy. It really *is* tragic. I'm afraid' – Julian Byrne lowered his voice as if a procession of enraged feminist mothers was about to invade his flat – 'I'm afraid that Teza was the most hopeless mother to the girl.'

Maldwin Carr raised his eyebrows in mock sternness. He was used to moral disapproval, usually of maternal functions improperly carried out, symbolizing a strong dislike for women. 'She didn't bring her up well,' he murmured, eyes chastely down as a priest in the confessional.

'Well?' Julian Byrne said, and this time the tones of Lady Bracknell could be heard in him. 'She never told her daughter who her father was. The girl, Mari, discovered only the other day that Ford really *was* her father. I mean, it was so egotistical of Teza – just because Ford left her years and years ago, she didn't feel she *had* to tell Mari about him.' Julian Byrne leaned forward once more, this time with a self-sending-up conspiratorial air. 'If Teza hadn't been at those endless meetings . . . You know what I mean.'

'So the girl is very disturbed?' Maldwin Carr said.

'Oh, yes. It was so sweet of her – she came to see me about three weeks ago, I suppose. She was distraught. She told me Ford was dead. But I don't see how she could possibly have known.'

'She told you that?' said Maldwin Carr in a different tone. Caution compelled him to keep still, while Julian Byrne's long fingers, stained amber from the many small cigars that made up his daily intake of nicotine, still fluttered in the air. 'Why do you think she wouldn't know?'

'Ford never communicated with her. She didn't seem to

know any friends of his either.' Julian Byrne shrugged. 'She said she'd had a dream. And, of course, the one thing she wants is to go out to St James and find her father's body and give it a proper burial.'

'Ah,' said Maldwin Carr.

'Antigone – rather touching,' said Julian Byrne. 'She may find him alive there, but I rather doubt it, you know.'

'I see.' Maldwin Carr rose to his feet. 'And she lives – in her mother's – in Teza's house, does she? Could you possibly give me the address?'

'Of *course* I will.' Julian Byrne, beaming, also rose to his feet. 'Poor Mari is absolutely penniless as well,' he said. 'Teza gives all her money to the Greenham women or something. It's rather marvellous of her – but poor Mari!'

'Oh, quite,' said Maldwin Carr quickly, as Julian Byrne scribbled down the street and number and handed it to him. 'I can't thank you enough for all your help.'

'I'll see you out,' said Julian Byrne, as the King Charles spaniel, sensing the rare opening of the door, went into a volley of barking from the old pantry. 'And do tell Mari to come and see me whenever she'd like to.'

The door was opened – quickly and jerkily – and Maldwin Carr guessed at his host's eagerness to be rid of him. Self-trained to exact information from the most unlikely sources, Maldwin patted his pocket and gave a mutter of annoyance. 'Too silly of me!'

'What?' Julian Byrne was right up close to him and caught off-guard. He wobbled on stork legs as Maldwin Carr pushed gently back past him into the sitting room.

'My pen,' Carr said, poking under the ottoman with a toe. 'Ah, here it is. Thank goodness. By the way,' he added as he went once more to the door and Julian Byrne, gyrating, became increasingly entangled in his own limbs, 'do you ever see Rex Spracker? I bumped into him the other day on the Underground.'

'Rex Spracker,' Julian Byrne said, as if reciting from an oculist's card.

'The militant Star Group chap. Friend of Ford. In that Black Power set-up with him and then disappeared. I was surprised to see him the other day, I have to admit. Now there's someone who one really would expect to be dead. It was like seeing a ghost of 1968.'

'I've no idea,' Julian Byrne said distantly, as if a parvenu, arriving for tea, had brought up the name of someone socially unacceptable.

'So Ford gave up politics?' Maldwin Carr said. He had been watching Julian Byrne closely while talking, and he saw that his words had produced, as he hoped they would, a fair amount of response. But at the word 'politics' the body of Julian Byrne straightened and the white hair shook vigorously.

'Ford was never properly serious about politics. He should have stuck to his early poetry. The last time I saw him – God knows how long ago it was – he told me he was thinking of joining the Ess Dee Pee!'

Julian Byrne's mocking laughter was long and shrill. Smiling in response, Maldwin Carr stepped backwards out of the antiquated flat and made his way down the stone stairwell. The laughter echoed behind him as he went.

The funny thing was [Lore wrote me in a letter that had 'Post Early for Christmas' on the envelope, which made me so homesick I nearly walked straight on to the *Singer*, which had brought over the weekly mail and sat there at the quay by the Coconut Bar like a bucket-shaped exit to freedom, London streets, rain and sanity] that when that strange guy Julian Byrne came round to see us I could have sworn he'd let himself in upstairs and had gone walking about in the sitting room, it must have been a few days before coming down the basement steps to ring our bell. You know, the boards let all the sound through, like with Teza's bloody meetings. And as soon as I saw him I realized he'd been hanging around on the street. But Teza was away, so I don't see how he can have. It spooked me a bit. Who's up to what? I keep thinking of stories of people breaking in and squatting a house before you can even tell the police.

Julian Byrne was kind to Mari, though, I must say. He came round a few days after a piece had appeared in the *Guardian*, saying Ford hadn't been seen lately and had he possibly been involved in the recent coup in Grenada. Julian Byrne came in and sat in my kitchen – he really is an odd fellow, Holly, do you remember him from the Green Velveteen? – and he said how fond of Ford he'd been and how he'd known him and Teza when they came over from St James and Ford started writing his poems. He was the first person to get *Dread Dance* and *Lond'n is a Singin' She-Dog* into print. He said he'd always wondered how Mari was, he'd last seen her when she was a tiny baby.

It was touching, I suppose. Mari is such a mixture of tough and vulnerable. I wish her own mother could see that and do something for her. (Teza's gone off to Cuba on a Women's International Conference or whatever, so maybe she'll pay you a flying visit.) Mari's eyes filled with tears. 'If only I could remember him,' she said to Julian. 'But I can't. I can't remember him at all!' And then there she was bursting into tears and Julian Byrne was comforting her in that very compelling voice he has, as if he's speaking fine lines to an audience. 'If only I could see him once,' poor Mari went on. 'Now I know for sure. About him being my father, I mean. D'you think he did go out to Grenada or St James and something . . . something happened to him?'

Holly, I could swear that man knows more than he'll let on. He said, 'He may have gone out there, Mari. He may well.' And she said, 'But why? Why would he put himself in such terrible danger?' And Julian Byrne said, 'If you believe in a cause, Mari, you find you have to do these things.' And she said, what cause was it? And he said, a cause which meant that the rich countries of the world wouldn't go on exploiting the poor Afro-Caribbean peoples. Mari looked very sad and proud at this – and then she said, surely the poetry was the important thing: it was better to stay home and write this beautiful poetry. Julian Byrne just shook his head, very decisively. I was a bit shocked, to tell the truth, because Mari is in a very thin-skinned state and everything Byrne said went straight in like gospel, just because he'd known Ford from his early days. 'How can poetry be as important as making a good life for people,' he said, 'as stopping imperialist aggression?' Mari nodded, she just sat there staring at him with her big eyes. I know it sounds cynical, Holly, but I wished at that moment that she'd never found out she was Ford's daughter. She was just starting a job on the local news-sheet reporting police assaults on the immigrant population, trouble at the West One Club, fires breaking out, old-age pensioners mugged – all that sort of thing. She'd been very happy doing that, and the editor said she could certainly string two words together. Now she thinks the gift for writing comes from Ford. She's sort of exalted and miserable at the same time. And if you take away the point of having a gift, which Julian Byrne did that day he came round, you're left with a very confused person.

'I'd really like to go out to St James and see it for myself,' Mari said. 'It's where I come from.' She looked angrily at me, as if I was her rejecting mother. (I think I'll have to clear out of here soon, Holly. Like you, I get stuck into places, that's the problem.)

'Yes, you should,' Julian Byrne said in a kind voice. 'Perhaps I can help you.'

'I haven't any money,' Mari said, going very red because it was clear Byrne had guessed that. 'I couldn't take from you – really – '

The long and short of it was that she didn't need to, and you may know that by now because she may be with you already. It was just such a strange succession of happenings. This man called Mal-something Carr comes round, and before you know where you are he says he's planning a cruise to the West Indies and would Mari like to come with him and cook? (I couldn't help laughing at that. The girl is bone-idle. Take-away kebab, pizza, hot dog, that's about all she'll go for, and she won't know how to fix those in the galley of a yacht.) And, as I say, this Carr man and Mari may have landed on your hibiscus shores by now, for all I know. But I get the feeling there's something very strange indeed going on.

Maldwin Carr was perfectly straight with Mari. He said he was a friend of Julian Byrne, or an acquaintance anyway. They'd met recently for a chat and Julian Byrne in passing had said that Mari was the daughter of the poet Ford and that there was nothing she wanted more than to go and find her roots in St James. And as he was planning this cruise – he had to write a book on some nomad tribe and he needed absolute tranquillity – why didn't Mari, etc., etc.?

Well, she fell for it, hook line and sinker. (Though just what she's falling for I don't yet know.) She changed colour like litmus paper. 'I'd really love to,' she said. Then she looked very sad again. 'I did dream a horrible dream,' she said, in such a low voice that neither Maldwin Carr nor I could clearly hear her. 'I dreamed my father was dead.'

Oh dear, Holly, it was all quite upsetting. I suppose Teza can't possibly know her daughter's gone to St James, not very far as a Hercules flies (as Teza would put it) from Cuba, where Teza is now.

By the way, what you say in your last letter about ordering a gun from the States – do take care, Holly. If only you came back here, I'd move out and we'd go back to a life like the old days, before all this funny political stuff and violence started to get into everything. First of all, I'd take you to the new Indian restaurant in Westbourne Grove. It's great – and they're very proud of their cinema ad that they have no flock wallpaper! Then we'd go back over to Chelsea and get some new boots. I wish you'd come.

'Describe my father to me,' Mari said as we stood in the store with Millie gone, swaying out up the hill with the Mediterranean goodies for Christmas dinner at Carib's Rest. 'Ford came back here the other day, didn't he, Holly? Just after the Americans went into Grenada. Had he changed a lot since you first knew him? Did he speak about me at all?'

No, you poor child, I nearly said. Ford walked in here looking young and fit. He wore a cream linen suit, exquisitely tailored: it was his way, no doubt, of making a joke against the Establishment, coming back to the island of his birth, ready to blow it up in the cause of freedom, and he'll dress posh for the part. No beret and jacket garb for he. He smiled at me. He gave me a kiss on the cheek. 'Here's my luggage, Holly,' he said. The big canvas bags followed him into the store. He smiled a wide smile.

'What's that, Ford?' I said. 'Where did you bring those bags from?' It was clear he'd bribed Mighty Barby, who always hangs around the quay when the *Singer* comes in, to carry the bags along the beach to the store for him.

'I've become a businessman,' Ford said. 'Export–Import. This is just a little bit on the Import side.'

Honestly, I don't know how he had the nerve. But he had charm all right. 'He was as charming as ever,' I said to Mari as she gazed at me like a young child made up sullen by a photographer for a shot but, under it all, shy and anxious, desperate even.

'The day Teza and he met,' Mari pleaded with me. 'Did they fall in love just like that?'

I said, 'Oh yes, they did.' But when I look back on it I can't remember anything special – when people are young they just seem to meet. Mari wouldn't ever be like that, I could see: Teza has spoiled her chances already.

'Ford, are you seriously asking me to look after these for you?' I said on that day he dropped in out of the blue. 'Suppose someone wants to open them and look inside? What's in there, and what about the customs?'

'I been through customs, man,' Ford said and he burst out laughing.

'But suppose you get caught?' I said, for I felt pretty sure by now. 'It's not worth it, surely?'

'There's my Holly,' says he, coming round the counter, pulling me out on to the floor of the store and giving me the once-over. 'Not so bad after all these years. I know where your heart lies, eh Holly? I sure I do!'

How d'you know I'm not middle-aged by now? I felt like saying. Revolution wears off – unless you're Teza, fixed in a zealous sisterhood which keeps you forever young. Maybe all the revolutionaries and reformers who've changed our lives for us are stuck in childhood that way. Maybe you have to be to keep your ideals. But I said nothing.

'Look, Holly, I'm leaving these here today and they'll be picked up tonight,' Ford said in a different voice, but still smiling. You could see him at a Buckingham Palace garden party. 'You'll leave the back door of the store open, Holly, like a good old lady.' Then he must have sensed something in me because he said, 'You're wondering why I trust you, Holly. Isn't that so?'

'Yes,' I said. 'I am.'

'Well, I'll tell you,' he said. 'It's pretty simple, really. There's no one else on this Godforsaken dump I can trust. Look at it that way.'

'But isn't it a terrible gamble?' I said.

'And when haven't I taken a gamble?' Ford said. 'Going

over to England that time, that was the first of them. One after the other ever since.' He shrugged his shoulders, elegant in the cream linen. 'And maybe this is the last of them,' he said.

'Your poetry,' I said, 'have you lost interest in that?'

'I ask you what that's for,' Ford said. The smile had gone out of his eyes. 'Lucky I have friends in London who put me back on the right path. And not the kind of friends you'd imagine, either!' Now he laughed again. I began to wonder – he was restless, pacing the store – if he was hipped on something. Or whether it was just his natural, reckless instinct, denied for years of novelty, and now a new game had come up.

I didn't tell Ford about Lore's letters, so I didn't tell him I knew about Julian Byrne, or that I'd known Byrne myself a little too when I worked at the Green Velveteen. He and Ford were like impatience and boredom coming together, and I couldn't think of anything more dangerous. 'I a-change de rules, I a-kill de blues', as the song has it. 'Even Castro condemned the New Jewel Movement,' I said, but I realized as I spoke that I sounded like an old colonel in Cheltenham or something.

Ford was confident; he'd made up his mind. He strolled to the back of the store and gave a loud whistle when he looked in at the Craft Centre room. 'Jeez, Holly, this is a tragic sight. What the fuck's goin' on here?'

I explained that the island had benefactors now in the guise of various Americans and Venezuelans from the consortium, and in particular one Jim Davy, who took all the trouble to set up a kiln and a weaving centre and so on in the village.

Ford laughed, but this time harshly. 'Caribbean peoples have no skills,' he said, 'no culture. We descended from slaves. What're our hands any good for?'

Firing guns, I thought, as I gazed at those damned canvas bags with an increasingly sinking heart.

'Not for making fancy pots!' Ford had suddenly exploded in anger. Then he quietened down again. 'I'll tell those friends who come to pick up my goods to be extra careful they don't break none of this valuable stuff when they come in the back door here.'

'Yes, do,' I begged him. 'God knows what some of the stuff is worth – one of those is a pre-Columbian urn.' For a moment Ford's expression went bright – and I remembered he'd been famous for his attempt in his poetry to wed the Mayan culture with the African tribal culture of his beginning. Then he shook his head quickly, as if a fly had flown in his eye. 'All I do know,' I went on, 'is that one hell of a lot of cash went into the accounts book for the Craft Centre a month ago. Nine million dollars. For a little local industry! I asked Jim Davy how the hell it got there and he said to ask no questions but to be glad for the future opportunities for St James!'

'Did he indeed?' Ford said. Then he gave me a walloping great pat on the back and said I was a good girl and he'd be back later. And off he went, into the blinding glare and the sand.

I had to lend the girl Mari a dress in the end, a white cheesecloth kind of thing. She'd swum over because she wanted to see me before she had to go up to the hotel, and she had nothing to wear.

I begin to see what Lore means. You have to start standing in as a mother for Teza whether you want to or not, and right now a mother is the last thing in the world that I'm aiming to be.

Then old Bratwurst in the golfing cap came into the store, and while I was still thinking this, the girl slipped away.

'So you couldn't say that it was definitely Ford who was shot down?' Maldwin Carr said. 'Whoever it was, doesn't it seem rather strange that the death went unreported?'

The girl Mari had joined the journalist on the verandah, and they sat on bamboo chairs facing Mrs Van der Pyck, who was the other side of a glass table. Between them long dishes of Smith's crisps flown from London to Barbados and then shipped on the *Singer* twice monthly in the high season for the nostalgia of cocktail drinkers at the hotel. A nest of whipped egg white, white rum and gardenia blossom in a glass bowl also separated them, and in the bowl were three straws, through one of which Mrs Van der Pyck sipped frequently. The girl's straw was untouched.

'Of course, I can't say I'm 100 per cent sure that anyone was actually *killed*,' Mrs Van der Pyck said. She threw a Beauty-of-the-Islands, high-cheekboned smile at Maldwin Carr: as soon as the girl from the yacht had arrived on the verandah she had known there was nothing going on there, and a more enjoyable Christmas Eve seemed to lie ahead. She even felt quite sorry for the girl, borrowing dirty Holly's dress – because she had no better, she could only suppose.

'We're interested because we're great admirers of Ford's poetry,' Maldwin Carr said in his gravest tones. 'The Poetry Society in London is extremely concerned that he missed a reading last month without giving notice. And that he failed to collect the Endeavor Prize in the States, of course. If by any chance Ford had decided to come out here at the time of crisis in Grenada . . .' Maldwin Carr's voice tailed off.

'Oh, I do see,' said Mrs Van der Pyck. She lowered her lips to the gleaming straw and ingested deeply, leaving a garotte mark of red.

Maldwin Carr then mentioned the name of the famous Sunday newspaper of which Lockton was proprietor. 'We're here to research the background of the poet,' he said, and he added that all Mrs Van der Pyck had to say would be treated with the utmost confidence.

'I was up at the pool,' said Mrs Van der Pyck. She waved a creamed and manicured hand in the direction of the expanse of blue, filtered water, laid out in the shape of a waterlily pad, which many of the guests preferred to the natural joys of the Caribbean. 'I saw a man run past. Hardly anyone runs here, you know, Mr Carr.' Another smile: it was clear from Mrs Van der Pyck's darting eyes that she was frightened. 'I don't want to exaggerate, you know. But it took me a second or two to realize that he wasn't running at all. He'd – well, I heard the shot but, you know, I thought it was Jim Davy starting up his silly old model plane, single-propeller thing he seems to have to shoot into before it'll get going – '

'You realized the man had been shot in the back,' Maldwin Carr said.

'Yes. And was sort of *flying* down the hill.'

'Into the sea,' Maldwin Carr said.

'Into the sea.'

Mrs Van der Pyck rose and went over to the rail of the verandah. Her gait was melodramatic and Maldwin Carr suppressed a smile. He wondered what Julian Byrne, after all the efforts he had made to persuade Ford to return to St James and thwart American presence in the West Indies, would make of the consequence: Ford missing presumed dead; a distraught daughter who had lost her father just as she found him; and a frivolous woman, red-hair-in-the-sun-set, commenting on it all in a voice heard too depressingly often at minor Embassy cocktail parties.

'It was all so terribly quick,' Mrs Van der Pyck said. She didn't add that a tumbler of vodka, fresh ginger and crushed ice had not helped her own progress to the side of the pool, where you can look down at the sea, the dilapidated store and the Bar. But she did say she had seen only the cloud of blood, in the water near the quay by the Bar, where it looked like it does if you cut your hand and pull the plug out of the basin, so there's a swirl and then it's all gone.

'You didn't see the man in the sea, then?' Maldwin Carr said. 'Where would the body have gone?'

Mrs Van der Pyck hesitated. Mari had risen too and had gone to stand looking out at the view: postcard coconut palms with a Day-Glo touch of pink round the fronds, scissoring a rusty sea.

Mrs Van der Pyck made up her mind. 'You really should ask Holly Baker about this,' she said. 'I'm pretty certain she was in the doorway of the store when the man . . . hurtled . . . past. In the back door, where they put the Crafts, you know.'

'Pretty certain,' Maldwin Carr said. His voice held the faintest note of derision: Mrs Van der Pyck was showing herself to be an unreliable witness – and on purpose too, he could sense. With a vague, aristocratic sweep of the hand Maldwin Carr knocked the three-day-old *Times* he had been pretending to read earlier to the verandah floor. With it, quite accidentally, went a saucer of nuts and crisps.

'Oh, I'm so sorry. What a bore,' said Maldwin Carr.

'If Holly *wasn't* there – the light was like this, you know, evening does set in so rapidly in this part of the world –' Mrs Van der Pyck was gabbling now. The slim young waiter from the inner room, hearing the crash of a glass dish, had come out on the verandah, and in the red light Mrs Van der Pyck saw Maldwin Carr's lizard eyes flicker over him. 'Or, as I say – I don't really remember about Holly, but there's one person who was *most* definitely on the hill just there as Ford . . . or whoever the poor man was . . . was shot down.' Mrs Van der Pyck gestured grandly at the hillside by the pool, almost green now in the dusk.

The waiter, crawling in the dark on the floor, retrieved a handful of crisps and replaced them on the saucer. Dark or not, Mrs Van der Pyck saw and stamped her foot in irritation.

'No, please! Throw them away!'

'Do tell us who it was,' said Maldwin Carr, much as though a crossword clue was about to be supplied unexpectedly.

'Sanjay.' Mrs Van der Pyck smiled, but her back was against the light and her face was invisible. 'Mr James Allard.

He was certainly down there. With his crazy daughter Pandora. You should go and see him, Mr Carr.'

Millie's left Carib's Rest. I can see her walk along the path on the side of the hill. She's going back to the village for a couple of hours before Christmas dinner gets under way. Down here I can smell the turkey and chestnut stuffing. Last year an English couple arrived with a bouquet of frozen chrysanthemums in a plastic sheath. To remind them of home, they said. You should have seen Sanjay's face light up, and then he looked sad again.

The day Ford was here. He left the store. I waited a while. I pulled down the plastic shutters so as to make the place look closed, and I could hear an Italian jet-set woman, a friend of the Venezuelans and a regular visitor, cursing outside on the blistering walkway when she found she couldn't get in for her fix of *marrons glacés*. And it didn't stop Jim Davy either from nipping in the back door to the Craft Centre. This time he was holding what looked like a hastily made clay bison, about six inches in length.

'My Johnny made this,' Jim said (he meant one of his pupils up at the village). 'It's great, isn't it, Holly? We're really making progress.'

I wish Jim Davy well, but he and his sort should go home. Let in the people from Grenada, I say, and let them teach the people of St James a different kind of craft: that of governing yourself instead of being told what to do by others. Look, I say to myself, Sanjay's lease runs out. Where will he go? What will he do? He likes the people of St James a sight more than he likes the consortium. Let him have the chance to let them in, so say I. Or so said I then. Now I just want one thing and that's peace. Next time the *Singer* comes I'm stepping aboard and I'll go to Trinidad and make my booking home. Lore'll get a surprise. We'll set up in Fulham, that's the place for us to be. A good distance from Teza anyhow.

When Jim had gone – and he seemed to take an age walking northwards up the beach, a beige ant in shorts and a visor cap with a face under it that looked as if it had been stamped out of a mould – when he'd turned twice to wave to me, I slipped out of the Craft Centre door and headed south. I knew Ford would have gone up to the village to say hello to Millie and the others. And I had to find Sanjay.

It was a long time since I'd walked out in the sun in the afternoon. My hair stuck to my head so fast it was like a pail of warm water had been emptied over it. My eyes, which felt like peeled eggs, kept blinking and rolling against their sockets. And the sand on the beach seemed as far away one moment as a photo map of the Sahara, where the fine ripples stretch out without perspective, and as near the next as a handful of grit pushed right up into your face.

The straggle of trees round the lagoon grew nearer all the same. I knew Sanjay would be in one of his derelict outbuildings: the library, where the peeling-off spines of the books hang like moths half out of their cocoons, or the aviary, where he opened the doors weeks ago and they all flew away – the humming birds and the mocking birds and the pelicans with their beaks like suitcases in the St Vincent street market. Or he'd be in the 'museum', where the clutter of old newspapers and pressed flowers and butterflies under broken glass has spilled over and almost smothered that effigy, in stone, of slavish love. I used to go in there, after Duchess Dora had died, and stare at the expression on the face of the woman, the mistress in the proper sense, of the man who had been called one hot afternoon to pass the afternoon in love under the shadow of the volcano at Pompeii. I thought of the lava falling on the slave and his owner. And I thought of this island, lying just under the shadow of Grenada, and the day coming when the violence would erupt and we'd all be frozen, for ever, in boiling stone.

Not that these thoughts do anyone much good. I had to tell

Sanjay that Ford was here. After sixteen years, a more successful gambler in life than Sanjay, whose enterprises had finally come to nothing back in London, Ford had turned up in a cream linen suit and with three bulging mailbags. 'Let's leave now,' I'd say to Sanjay as we stood watching some of his favourite birds – red-legged partridges from St Lucia – as they flew in over the reef and settled on the scratchy lawn. 'Let's take a small boat out, like Teza and Ford, all those years ago. We'll row over to Union Island and change to a big cruise liner in Trinidad and go all the way down to Tierra del Fuego. Walk away from the place and they'll thank you because they're coming over tonight.'

I walked through the thinnest part of the jungle and then through a plantation of coconut palms that were as straight as stripes on a wallpaper and then into the riot of bushes and trees that protects Sanjay's house from the outside world. There'd been a sudden, rare downpour this morning, and the too-bright grass belched up steam at me. I went on, knowing as I went that the house didn't have Sanjay in it. I can tell when he's around. And, of course, I hadn't got used to the fact that his daughter Pandora was back with him since a few days before, after the bombing of the Grenada madhouse. I felt something – heard something – on the verandah, and for a moment I was afraid because it sounded like Duchess Dora's rocking-chair when she was ill and sat all day on the verandah, rocking, rocking. But it was only poor Pandora; she was humming a sort of tuneless hum. And Tanty Grace was beside her on an upright chair by a rickety table with wools and a needlework frame.

Our mad girl, Pandora. I turned and went silently down to the lagoon. For I knew Sanjay must be there. He never goes up to the north now. So there was, literally, nowhere else he could be.

It's silly, though, to think you can walk past Tanty Grace and Pandora without them seeing you. The first thing that happened was that I stumbled against a root – a tree felled in the preparations for the airport, a disturbing sight – and I gave a hissing breath that must have sounded loud, in the stagnant air. There was a clatter behind me on the verandah, as if Pandora had risen clumsily and sent the shaky table over. Then, trying to go on, I found myself wading through a heap of white feathers, half-hidden under a tamarind tree.

No one who hasn't lived out in these parts can know what the sight of that pile of white cock's feathers can mean. If they'd a hunch – that is, that if the feathers didn't mean anything to them – they'd have no reason to feel fear. I knew. I'm not likely to forget the feathers in Tanty Grace's yard, three houses down from Millie in the village.

I only wanted a few days – or weeks, or maybe a year – of a kind of happiness only Tanty Grace knows how to get for you.

Of course, Dora'd been ill a long time with one thing or another. And when she died it was of real fever. But that day, when Ford came and I went looking for Sanjay and I walked into that circle of feathers that looked as if Tanty Grace had set it right there under the trees, I thought again I heard Dora in the rocking-chair and heard its groan. No one really expected Dora to die. And Sanjay took it so bad. There's been some *obeah* woman working against her, he said. His face was dark with grief and rage. I remember I lifted my rum punch – we were always in the Bar and he drank himself silly those days, trying to get over it all – and I remember too that the glass was frosted outside, with the ice melting so fast your fingers left a clear trail like a snail's. I must have concentrated on that so as not to feel too glad.

That was four years ago. She's well dead by now. A year after the new régime started up in Grenada, 'I shan't go and see Pandora in the asylum any more,' she said. 'They don't want me to visit, I don't like the atmosphere on that island any more.' And Sanjay said, well, he would because he loved his daughter so much, even if she didn't have the faintest idea of who he might be when he came. And some of Sanjay's birds escaped that year, I remember, because I saw their feathers too.

It was Maldwin Carr's intention to visit the village before he went down to the house by the lagoon, but first he took the girl Mari over to the yacht for a change of clothes, and he found it hard to restrain himself then from asking her what the lady who ran the store might have found to say on the subject of Ford. Restrain himself, however, he did: Maldwin Carr could see the girl was in a highly charged state, very unlike the cool, almost detached manner she had assumed on the long plane flight to Barbados and the subsequent trip down to the Grenadines. In Maldwin Carr's impassive features caution and calculation combined, and by the time the Boston Whaler, which accompanied the yacht, had drawn up alongside, he was no more than a concerned employer, helping a young lady up the gangway and calling out for another hand from the crew.

A radio message had arrived for Maldwin Carr while he had been supping his gardenia-laden drink on the verandah of Carib's Rest. It informed him that a certain Mr Jim Davy was expected to arrive that evening, Christmas Eve, on the island. Maldwin Carr should exchange such information as he had gleaned with Mr Davy, who would make contact with him at dinner at the hotel.

The foreign editor of Lockton's newspaper hoped Maldwin Carr was enjoying his trip and then signed off. And Maldwin Carr, who seemed as certain of arriving at trouble spots at the right time (or the wrong time, depending on how you looked at it) as did Young Lochinvar when he Rode Out of the West to arrive at the wedding of his love to another, smiled faintly to himself before going to his cabin and donning the shark-skin dinner jacket that was *de rigueur* for a Christmas celebration at Carib's Rest.

As the girl showered and changed, Maldwin Carr reflected on the speed with which the transactions between them had been completed. It was as if, when he had arrived at the house off the Portobello Road to pay his visit to Teza (as he had thought, but another woman who called herself Eleanore had been the one to let him in), Julian Byrne had already informed Ford's daughter of this opportunity to go out to St James and look for her father; and Maldwin Carr had no doubt that he had. It was hardly difficult to imagine the instructions Mari had been given on arrival at the island – the only wonder, Maldwin Carr thought, was that she and her friend Eleanore had so easily swallowed his story of needing a cook and of having the girl's interests at heart in taking her on a cruise in the West Indies. She must, by now at least, have noticed that the 'crew', a man well used to preparing food, had done precisely that throughout the journey; that she was, in that respect at least, useless. Yet she seemed quite unmoved: it was her age, he supposed, or perhaps the sense of her mission that made her oblivious to these primary things.

When Mari came into the neat, teak-fitted cabin where Maldwin Carr sat waiting, he suppressed a smile at her appearance – a West London get-up of corkscrewed hair and layered rags and a baggy blouse – and suggested a drink. Mari shook her head. Not for the first time, Maldwin found himself amused by the need for a look of fury in today's young. But then, remembering his liberal views, he silently conceded that unemployment and the prospect of a futureless world might permit a certain measure of fury. He stepped up on deck and held out an arm to help the girl down once more to the speedboat that would take them to the quay – and perhaps a quick visit to the Bar – before going on up to the village.

'You think Ford is dead, don't you?' Mari's voice was close behind him. He turned to find her already on deck and glowering under a moon that seemed twice the normal size.

'I don't know, Mari, dear,' Maldwin said. 'Surely that's one of the things we've come to find out.' He was aware of the tired cynicism of his tone – so he told Jim Davy much later, when he looked back on the events of the evening – but he hadn't been ready for the outburst, after the week they'd spent in near-silence together, or for the hatred of which the girl showed herself to be capable.

'You're all in it together, aren't you?' she cried. (The 'crew', waiting down at the wheel of the Boston Whaler, looked carefully out to sea.) 'You and Julian Byrne and this "Sanjay" and Holly and all of you! It's a plot. I tell you, baby, I know a set-up when I see one!'

For a moment Maldwin Carr could have sworn that the girl's face changed entirely. She was angry but in an arrogant way he hadn't thought possible from her. In the moonlight she was white, and her hair, braided out from her head, was a deep black.

'What are we all in?' said Maldwin Carr quietly. (Across the water more lights in the Bar went on. Flashes of phosphorescence lit up the small waves, and the 'crew' leaned over towards them from the side of the boat.)

But the girl was laughing. It started as a harsh, made-up laugh, then she did it for proper – head back, shoulders convulsing under the junky old blouse, a beautiful neck, very long and slim, bending and swaying with the sheer volume of the laugh.

'We're in nothing, you know,' said Maldwin Carr. 'Please, Mari, shall we go?' (For by now he felt a sudden chill: the girl had gone off her head, maybe, or was heavily on drugs. He would take her up to the hotel, pursue his inquiries alone.)

'Julian Byrne, Maldwin Carr, Sanjay, Holly and me,' the girl cried, still choking with laughter. 'My God, man. Give me five!' And she calmed as suddenly as she had begun. 'You go nowhere without me,' she said, eerily echoing Maldwin's most recent thoughts. 'And don't you think you can slip away from me so easy, Mr Carr. 'Cos I'll be after you.'

Maldwin Carr cleared his throat, a signal to the man in the boat below to rev the engine. He had to admit, he said to Jim Davy as they later ran together to the south of the island and it was Maldwin's chore to explain how the girl had slipped away from him, that he had never in his life before witnessed so rapid a facial change in anyone. For as they went down the ladder to the boat that would take them to shore, she turned once and looked back at him. And she was a different person again, Maldwin Carr said. Caught between the side of the yacht and the dark water, her face was black, features heavy in her face, mouth full in a savage contempt. Her plaited hair was like reeds in a tribal crown. From then on he'd known that he'd lose sight of her, that she'd change herself and slip from his fingers and away however hard he tried to keep her in his sights.

At first, though, the girl's rage seemed to have cleared the air. By the time the small boat was at the quay, she was smiling – almost, anyway, thought Maldwin as he shot uncomfortable glances at her in the stern. She stepped out, and there they were on the jetty and then on the soft white sand where dug-out canoes and fishermen's boats were pushed up – boats like the one Ford and the girl's mother had eloped in, Maldwin thought, and then he felt uncomfortable again. It was a few seconds' walk along to the Bar, and he tried to sense her mood as they went. But the fronds of palm came down in zebra-stripe shadows over her face, and she was as remote as an actress in an ancient film: flickering, silent, an image in chiaroscuro. They reached the side steps to the Bar and walked up. Bunting had been strung across and fairy lights that looked as if they had been pulled out of the bargain basement of an Oxford Street store. Rolling Stones on the jukebox – 'Satisfaction'. And only two people there: the Negro albino boy Maldwin had glimpsed on the beach when he arrived, doing press-ups, and a woman, blowsy-looking rather, shaking thin silver bangles like the bangles hippies used to wear that tinkled and crashed as they passed each other a joint. This woman, Maldwin Carr ascertained, was the woman who ran the store.

'Pathetic, aren't they?' Holly waved at the decorations. Maldwin backed slightly: he was fastidious and sensed spit, bad teeth, rum and a daub of toothpaste on top. 'They're Sanjay's – he had them as a child. Not here, of course.'

'No, of course,' muttered Maldwin. 'I knew . . . er . . . Sanjay slightly when he was younger, actually. We were at the same school. And then I used to see him and . . . er . . . Dora in London before they came out here.'

'How simply fascinating,' said Holly Baker coldly. She turned to the girl, who was standing with her eyes fixed on her as if Holly were capable, with some extraordinary conjuring trick, of pulling her missing father, dead or alive, out of a hat. And indeed she may be, thought Maldwin Carr. She knows what happened to him. Or where he is.

'We were thinking of paying a visit to Sanjay,' Maldwin said. 'I believe the hotel has a car. D'you think we could borrow it and drive down there?' He pointed to the lagoon. 'That *is* where he lives, isn't it?' he said.

Holly Baker told Maldwin that he had only to go up to the hotel and ask. It was none of her business what happened up there. No, she would not be at the Christmas dinner tonight. How kind of Mr Carr, but she was quite unable to accept. No doubt she'd see him later, back here at the Bar. Dinner at Carib's Rest wasn't for the likes of her, no man, you bet, and she stay here, Holly will, until it's time to pick up she cutlass an go.

Maldwin Carr looked mildly surprised. But he could tell already the dislike of his class and gender sizzling out of the woman in the old Indian printed caftan, under which poked dirty feet in thonged sandals – a hatred that grew up strong again in the girl, it was plain to see. Holly, after all, was the old friend of Teza. These women stood, arms akimbo, against the world. The world made by men, as they saw it (though the strong personality of Lady Anthea Carr had caused her son to think, until he went to private school anyway, that women were solely responsible for the making of the world). The schism between the two women and the man widened as the disc on the jukebox shrieked to a close. There was no noise now except the slap of waves against the posts holding up the floor of the bar. In the centre of the small dance floor Mighty Barby executed a few headstands.

'We'll go up to the village first,' Maldwin Carr said to Mari, 'and then on to visit Mr Allard before dinner at the hotel. We'll borrow the car.'

'You can give me a lift,' Holly Baker said.

Maldwin Carr said he'd be delighted. Holly said she didn't live in affluent circumstances. Her place was laughingly called The Heights and was down the other side of the hill beyond the village. Where they didn't manage to clear all the mosquitoes. Wrong side of the tracks. But she'd pick up her things from the store and be waiting for them in the road. It was time she told them a few things, she said, as it looks like they are getting their facts just a tiny bit wrong.

Out of here, out of the store, for a few days at least. Even at St James they don't expect you to stand behind the counter Christmas and Boxing Day. And out of the store – what for? The grey room with the cockroaches down at The Heights. The patchwork counterpane where I lie with my hand up inside my legs and it's hot and dry there, like July, waiting for the hurricanes and the rain and you think they'll never come – and when they do, the hot mud and the sad skies and Millie walking from the village to the hotel with her head down and rain running in her breasts like it was a drainpipe there. What for? But I'll go back one more time. With the posh gentleman who needs a good kick up the arse, and that silly girl who wants her hair pulling out by the screws. Then I'll be off. Late tonight, when they're all drunk in the Bar and the guests at Carib's Rest have gone back to their gingerbread cottages. And while they stand undressing by the window in the moon and look out at the merriment still going on in the long cottonhouse room. And when there's that sickening smell in the air of the old slave plantations. Then – then I'll take one of the fishermen's boats and I'll go. I might get as far as Carriacou. They'll pick me up. My photo'll be in all the papers, and not before time.

Late October, when Ford came, I still believed I meant something here. When he'd left the store, and I walked down to the lagoon in that incredible heat, I thought I could make Sanjay understand. 'This place is over for you – and for me,' I said. 'All we have to do is go.'

But he just stood staring at me by the side of the lagoon. He'd found one of those pieces of driftwood that look as if some animal's turned to wood and lived underwater, to come washing up hundreds of years later through a hole in the reef. He held it up at me. 'Squirrel, Holly?' he said. 'Or racoon?'

I wasn't having any, though. 'Ford's here,' I said. 'He's come to get his friends over from Grenada. They'll blow up the place. Just thought you might like to know.'

Sanjay looked at me as if I was something even odder that had washed in to the stewpot of the lagoon. 'Ford?' he said. 'After all these years?' He looked pleased and excited. 'I'd really love to see Ford,' he said, but he sounded wistful, as if he knew already that there wasn't a chance. 'How is he looking?' Sanjay said. 'I'd like to tell him I admire his poetry.'

'Forget his poetry,' I said. 'Ford has been through the poetry stage. And he's not writing soul cookbooks like the Black Panthers these days either. He's in with revolution. And you're the target.'

Sanjay's innocence was pitiful to see. Boy, won't he get what's coming to him. I'll be the survivor, pick up me cutlass an go. Or the gun. Didn't Jim Davy say he'd bring me back a Colt .22 from the States? And where's Jim Davy now, just when he's needed, I'd like to know?

'Me?' said Sanjay.

'Yes, you,' I said. 'Ford wants to take over the whole island with his friends.'

'His friends?' said Sanjay in a pained tone, as if a party by a naughty child was threatening to get out of control.

'He's brought arms,' I said. 'Whoever's not in gaol of the Marxist-Leninist group in Grenada, they're the ones he'll supply with arms when they land tonight. Julian Byrne put him up to it.'

Sanjay threw back his head and laughed aloud. 'Julian Byrne? But that's ridiculous. The man of letters?'

'Now the man of left-wing takeovers,' I said. 'Look, Sanjay, your lease runs out in the New Year. Why don't you just walk away from all this, I mean, start again . . . somewhere?'

Sanjay put his hands up in the air as if he was practising for being put up against the wall and shot. The piece of grey driftwood dropped tail-first into the sea.

'I can't, Holly!' he said.

'You can't,' I said after him. We stood there by the side of the lagoon. There was a bit of shade, not much, from the manchineel trees. Quite a lot of them had been cut down already to make an approach to the new runway.

'I can't leave Pandora,' Sanjay said.

I don't know, but my patience just ran out. For God's sake, he could take her too. But I didn't even bother to say it. I knew it wasn't just Pandora. It was the whole part of his life that she stood for: his life on the island when she was a little child, which was all she could know, as her mind had been cloudy so long. And so that time was always present for Sanjay in her. He couldn't leave. He was as much chained to the place as an indentured labourer.

'Very well,' I said. 'I'll go. But keep safe in your bed tonight.'

And I did go, as far as the plantation of palms and past the pile of feathers that looked as if they'd been disarranged since I'd come down to the lagoon, and on to the emerald lawn, which in the sun had already stopped exhaling vapour. That was as far as I went – although I did get back to The Heights in the end and waited till the next day to hear the complaints about the sudden closing of the store. I mean, I didn't have it in me to step into a boat – not then.

Lore had a postscript on her last letter.

I feel really sorry for Mari now [she scrawled]. Listen, Holly, you better do something about this. I've seen the girl grow more and more pale and agitated over the past few days – and so I decided to follow her – yesterday, that is. It's bitterly cold, right? Teza's just sent a Christmas card – it isn't a real one like Mari would secretly have wanted, with reindeer and snow and all that. No, it's a card from Cuba with Fidel's picture and a long speech in Spanish on the back – and the card coming means Teza won't be home for Christmas because she says so in so many words. 'Oh never mind,' I say, 'why don't we have a nice little party here together in the basement? You invite some of your friends. Then we'll go to Covent Garden and see the break-dancing.' I can tell you, it was the last thing I wanted to do. Mari's friends she was at

Holland Park with, are quite nice kids and all that, but it makes me feel pretty old and dreary when I haven't seen a man in God knows how long. It must be something to do with being a surrogate mother, I suppose. It puts them off.

Anyway, Mari said she didn't want a party. 'Come on, girl,' I said. 'Cheer up. Teza wouldn't have organized anything better for you anyway.'

As soon as I said that, of course, I could have bitten my tongue out. Tears started to roll. Then, when she'd quietened down a bit, Mari said: 'Neither of my parents loves me. And that's good.'

'What the hell d'you mean?' I said.

'The family,' Mari said. 'It's the nucleus of evil.'

'Oh come on,' I said. 'And where do you get all that from?' But of course I know by now that this stuff has been current jargon practically since Mari was born. R. D. Laing elaborates on that well-known Larkin line, 'They fuck you up, your mum and dad', and next thing you've got a lot of loonies wandering about free on the streets. 'Who've you been seeing?' I said. Mari just 'brickwalled', as I've heard desperate parents of teenagers describe the process, as they queue for veg in the market.

Mari stayed quiet all of that day (the day before yesterday) and next morning she thought she'd slipped out of the house without being seen because I heard the front door shut ever so quietly. It took me a minute or two to get dressed. Then I went after her.

Blow me if it hadn't snowed in the night. I've no good boots and no money to afford a proper pair. (You must've saved a pile by now, Holly. Life'd be much cheaper if you came over and we shared a flat.) At least the snow helped me to follow Mari – that's the funny part – it was like a fairy story. She's got pretty big feet and she'd left a trail down the street. No one else was up yet. I caught her up on the corner of Portobello Road, buying hot chestnuts off a man with a pile of embers. 'Go away, Lore,' she said. 'Mind your own business. Please!'

'No, I won't,' I said. 'You're up to no good and I know it.' It's funny how you turn into your own grandmother, once you have dealings with a young girl like her. 'I'm coming with you,' I said, 'or I'm sending a cable to Teza to say I can't cope with the scene here and she's got to come home.'

Mari hesitated: I knew that would count all right.

In the middle of a conference, I said weightily. 'Just think of it, Mari.'

It worked, of course. Mari strode off in her babyish snow-boots and I followed. The crescents round Ladbroke Grove were all sparkling with fresh snow, and in the communal gardens behind Julian Byrne's flat there were children in red scarves and leg warmers making a great nest of snow and falling about in it. We turned into the hallway and Mari walked up without looking back, as if she'd decided I simply wasn't there. And, sure enough, when she rang the doorbell and Julian Byrne came out in a silk-patterned dressing gown like that man in *Private Lives*, he seemed to consider I was invisible too. I haven't often had the door slammed in my face (except the time I went to the all-gay party by mistake and they said hang on a minute when they thought I was a drag queen and then when they saw I wasn't they shoved me out and banged the door shut) and when Julian Byrne slammed on me I was so shocked I couldn't believe it for a good few seconds, I can tell you. I mean, Holly, you and me and Byrne used to exchange jokes, 'bad-to-worsinage', d'you remember, at the Green Velveteen? And then he's been hanging about our street and I've seen him whisk round the corner into the market several times in the past few weeks – and I know he's seen me too. What the hell is he up to? I thought often enough. You know, it crossed my mind that Byrne planted that photo of Ford and the ring and all that in Teza's drawer for Mari to find. He's using her, no doubt about that. But I can't say anything to Mari, she'd blow up in my face. And I've no proof. But Byrne is a fox – and he's planning to eat her. And the worst part of it is that poor Mari is the silly duck – or goose, if you like – and doesn't know it.

I took up my position by the door. It was freezing cold on the stone landing, and I almost thought I'd go home and to hell with it when I had my first stroke of luck. A cleaning woman, a friendly type, came up the stairs. 'Poor dear, are you locked out?' she says, and before I knew where I was I had gained admittance to the great man's abode! And while the cleaner went into the kitchen and started crashing round with the remains of our revolutionary Mr Byrne's Dover sole dinner (I saw the remains in the waste bucket by the larder), I was able to stand right up against the door of the sitting room and hear everything, or nearly, that was going on!

There were two men in there as well as Julian Byrne and Mari. One sounded young and – probably – Australian. He kept saying, 'That's great, Mari, really great.' But I couldn't make out what 'that' was. Another man had a more muted, precise voice. He sounded a bit, well, frightening to me. The first thing he said was, 'We're not able to give any guarantees, as I'm sure you must realize. It's what Ford would have wanted.' And Mari said, 'Yes, yes,' as if she was giving responses at the marriage altar or something. Then Julian Byrne spoke up. You can't miss *his* voice anyway! It's like an actor sending up a camp voice and then getting tired of it halfway through and going straight. Anyway, you remember, Holly. Somehow everything he says sounds funny. I had to stifle a giggle all right.

'Mari, you mustn't get even *faintly* over-excited,' Julian said, 'but there's a very strong possibility that your father may still be alive.'

You could hear poor Mari gasp. At that very moment the cleaner dropped a water jug in the kitchen and the King Charles spaniel went off into a volley of barks, so I missed what came next – but Julian Byrne was ending with something like, 'That woman who came here with you, Mari, that dreadful woman – she didn't get in here, did she?' And his voice was much sharper than usual.

'No no, she'll have gone home,' Mari said. And she must have reached out and stopped Julian from going and flinging open the door and exposing me there because she said in an urgent tone, 'Please, Julian, please, for God's sake, tell me if Ford is alive in St James.'

'He's not in St James right now,' said the Australian voice. 'He wants to go back there, though.'

'You can let him in,' said the muted voice. It was a voice used to giving quiet instructions, and I had to lean right down to the keyhole to hear. Needless to say, the keyhole had a bloody great key in it, and I couldn't hear better at all.

'Let him in?' poor Mari was saying as I straightened up again. 'But how?'

Byrne was a little less patient this time. He said to Mari that she must have been surprised and pleased, to say the very *least*, when a charming gentleman turns up just at the time he's needed and offers to take her to the island of her origins. 'It was no accident,' Julian said. 'I put him on to you, Mari, my dear. He considers you to be very useful to him in his search for your father. He believes you will lead him straight to the spot marked X, if you know what I mean.'

'But why should this Mr Carr man want to find Ford?' says Mari.

And the Australian pipes up now with, 'Where have *you* been all your life?'

And Julian Byrne says, 'Rex, please, restrain yourself,' or something of the sort.

'Mr Carr is employed by a certain Sunday newspaper. The proprietor has interests in that part of the world,' Byrne went on, enjoying himself again. 'They've heard trouble may be brewing in a few . . . er . . . neighbouring islands, and they want to stop it before it gets under way. They want to find Ford . . .'

Mari broke in here. I think it was the first time she saw herself as a pawn and she started to struggle a bit. But to expect facts to be plain and straightforward was mad, of course. Byrne simply said in a soothing voice that she'd already been told not to expect guarantees. They couldn't be sure of anything. But what they'd heard was that if Mari could go to the southern tip of the island – there was a lagoon there apparently, and it was a bit of a jungle, but a track had been cleared recently for a new airport – and stand right on the tip by the reef and show a light . . .

'That's where Ford'll come if he's coming at all,' said the Australian and Byrne and the quiet man all together.

'And please lose Mr Carr in the course of the evening,' said Julian Byrne with a laugh. 'It'll be Christmas Eve. He'll probably get lovely and drunk – if you help him, of course.'

'But suppose he's heard too that something . . . might happen on that night?' said Mari, showing more intelligence than I'd credited her with. 'He won't go and get drunk or anything. He'll stick with me all the time!' And I felt sorry for her again, Holly. The wretched girl was beginning to realize she was in something big and impossible to escape from and they had her where they wanted her, of course.

'You needn't go,' said Julian in his kindest voice.

'No!' said Mari, terrified.

Then the young Australian started to speak. 'You know what they're doing on that island?' he said. 'They're pumping in dollars to keep the islanders in a state of subjugation. They're building up caches of arms to murder the St Jamesians if they do rise up with the aid of the comrades. They're introducing biological warfare. A breed of mosquito that's never been reported outside Africa has suddenly appeared on those islands. There are deaths resulting. Outbreaks of dengue fever. Trees shedding their leaves and dying. All to keep their capitalistic enterprises on the go.'

After this schoolboyish speech, which had obviously made Mari colour up the way she does – she's a real little Turk when it comes to 'fair' and 'unfair' and all that, because she said, 'That's disgusting. *God!*' – there was a scraping back of chairs and I saw I had to slide back along the wall and get to the front door. The cleaner was safely off in a far bedroom.

No more to report, Holly – I was out and down the stone stairs and in the crescent where the snow had iced over even more and the sun was shining and it was pretty as a Christmas card. The thing is, Holly, I feel worried for *you* now as well as for the girl. For God's sake, what shall I do? Should I send a cable to Teza after all?

When I'd been home about half an hour Mari let herself in and smiled at me quite kindly. 'I'm sorry to shut you out, Lore,' she said. 'But you don't mind really, do you?' And she took off her tatty old cloak and came and sat on the rug at my feet. She's got a cheek, Holly, honestly she has. 'I have to go and see Julian sometimes,' she said. 'He tells me things.' And I must say, she looked radiant.

'What kind of things?' I said, although I knew perfectly well, of course.

'He told me my real name was Marina,' she said. (After I'd slipped out, I suppose, and he'd started pulling all the emotional strings.)

'Ford loved the name, Julian told me. He said it was the name of a lost daughter who wandered over the seas and then got reunited with her father in the end, when he thought she'd been drowned all that time.'

'How very poetic,' I said.

Lore added that she'd decided to spend Christmas with her mother in Torquay. Then she signed off, with all the usual pleas for me to come over soon.

I'll take that Maldwin and the girl up to The Heights and I'll give them one more chance to get off the island. 'You're in danger,' I'll tell that stiff-necked man who looks as if he's seen too many spy movies. 'Mari, go home,' I'll say, 'or you may regret it all very much indeed.'

I'll have to go down to the lagoon. That's me, poor Holly, you see there, trudging down past the scratchy bushes on the bone-dry track in the dark with a torch in one hand and a spade in the other. Because I know what Mari's being sent to do even if she doesn't, poor girl.

What I say is, fair is fair, let 'em come. But don't let 'em get at the guns. How about that one, Lenin?

But that won't get anyone very far. In Grenada, the island next door, everything belongs to the people these days. The sad part is that the people here don't know that nothing belongs to them at all.

Racing on, meandering on in the hotel jeep, I can hardly stop myself from falling out as we bump up and over the top of the hill. There's Millie, coming out of her house in a fresh cotton dress. She'll tie on her apron when she gets to Carib's Rest, she'll cook the Christmas dinner and then help serve it up. I don't know how she stands for it here. But then, when you look at any of our lives, I don't know how I do either.

There's Tanty Grace now, as the hotel jeep slows, and Mr Maldwin Carr says perhaps they should stop and ask a few questions first in the village, and I say, 'No, go on. I want to go home straightaway.'

Tanty Grace sets out at the same pace as Millie. I watch them in the side mirror of the jeep. All the feathers and all the spells. And it was the Americans after all who put in that mosquito that gave Dora the dengue fever so she died. There's enough evil in the world without whistling for it.

Tanty Grace and Millie'll leave the row of houses together.

At the foot of the hill, where there's a beautiful tree with pink blossom like a wedding – I've never found out its name – they'll go off in separate directions: Millie to the cranberry sauce and crackers with ribald jokes that came down last month on the *Singer* from Barbados, Tanty Grace to another grim evening sitting with poor mad Pandora and trying to make sure she doesn't put her finger down her throat and bring up the pills she has to take to control her terrible visions. Then Sanjay will be drinking on the verandah. Sometimes a big moth will bang into his face and he won't even bother to brush it off, as if it might be a fragment of a bad dream he was having anyway.

That day Ford came, I went back past the house over the billiard-table-green grass, and the feathers under the trees on the way made me remember Tanty Grace, and I thought of how I'd tried her spells. Then the next day, when I came back to the store (Ford's bags had gone, of course), I remembered Sanjay's messenger birds and Jim Davy saying it was his hobby to teach them to fly from one island to another – and he said, laughing, 'You have to put salt on their tails, you know, Holly.' But now I know it was poison, really. Those birds were being trained to fly to Grenada. And my feathers never hurt Dora at all.

Dora came from a family in West Cork. She liked the rain and the grey skies. She hated it here. The wrong sea, the wrong colour – everything about the place depressed her. Even the fruit and the flowers were too big. 'They look like the photo of the wax flowers on my grandmother's bonnet at Schull fair,' she said. How she loved her family! They'd intermarried with the other couple of families that came over to settle estates in Ireland from England in the seventeenth century, much as the Allards had done here. They were more like poor whites, though; they didn't have the Allards' mercantile sense that went on down the generations until you get to Sanjay throwing it all away. They sounded like those mean whites in Barbados, who came over from the West Country at the time of the Monmouth rebellion and stayed poor and half-mad with the interbreeding, farming their little scraps of land. 'Redlegs', they call them. Dora was a bit of a redleg, I used to think. There was her ancient line in Ireland and the grey stone house with the roof coming off, and the parties in London when she'd come over from Ireland, and she was so pretty Sanjay married her without thinking twice. But she had a funny, dopey look. Her big blue eyes were set too close together. No wonder she and Sanjay made a mad child. No wonder, with all that interbreeding.

I used to think, when I wandered down to the lagoon on those evenings that were too hot to get through alone, that Sanjay had something a bit missing too, as he sat hour after hour in his museum or carving grotesque animals out of driftwood. It was a pity he gave up making his boats. The perfect mast. Sails that fluttered so clean and delicate, when he was likely to go around in a dirty shirt and forget to change unless Millie whipped it away from him. A galleon with a hundred tiny oars. I knew that one was a slave ship, and Sanjay was embarrassed he'd made it but he just couldn't resist it for the sheer beauty of the thing. And I'd put my hammock up in the pleasant clearing of nutmeg and cacao trees that stretches away to the southernmost tip of the island and watch Sanjay encouraging the children to build the harbour out of stones and those big pink shells the colour of old-fashioned knickers. And a little quay – the mud cement-mixing was their favourite part. I liked to watch the bend of his shoulders and back, as he worked on repairs to the fleet or pencilled a small skull and crossbones on a handkerchief to amuse a child.

It's true that that's where I'll go tonight, and it's true too that although the small harbour's all grown over with jungle and Dora died from a terrible fever just about the time Grenada changed direction and Pandora's back here as helpless as a baby, nothing's really changed. Sanjay is the landlord, for another week at least.

Poor Dora. She'd be miserable now if she saw me drive in the jeep up to The Heights with just the kind of man she would have found glamorous and respectable and a honey-skinned girl who gets so black with silent rage she vanishes into the darkness in the front seat by the driver. How Dora would have hated her! And how she'd have hated to see me take these new guests into my squalid room and tell them everything they want to know. Yes, and go down to the lagoon later and dig for the guns Ford must have left there. She wouldn't have liked to find me so in charge of her home – even if she never was happy here. 'St James is my island,' she said to me once, when I'd left neutral ground by the store and was playing Tom Tiddlers on the beach down by the lagoon. 'Holly, why don't you go back to where you belong?'

Of course I shouldn't really have said to the girl what I did. But everything can be corrected. 'Everything can be made shipshape again,' as Sanjay used to say when the little kids blundered about on the pretend jetty and the wet mud fell in near his precious fleet.

'So you're another person who can't remember exactly whether the man you saw shooting down the hill and into the sea was a man you knew or a perfect stranger,' said Maldwin Carr with quiet sarcasm. He was on a rush chair – the only chair in the room – under a light bulb inadequately covered in stained parchment, so the light was bright in the eyes, uncomfortably like an interrogation room and made no more agreeable by the way the girl had taken up a deliberately martyred position on the floor on a rug so old and dirty it looked like the ends of a hundred mops sewn together. Holly stood by the side of the bed, arms folded over a stomach that ran sideways under her arms in ripples of fat. Why does the woman have to live in quite such miserable surroundings? Maldwin thought, and he noted this thought, from pure impatience, from habit, on the school pad that he carried always with him and that emerged, invariably to the surprise of onlookers, from his elegant suit. There was something self-pitying and attention-seeking in this statement of poverty, Maldwin Carr decided. 'Find who she's trying to get to feel sorry for her,' he scribbled down. 'Allard? Probably.'

The notepad went on to record that Ms Holly Baker had spent an inordinate amount of time talking about the trials and tribulations suffered by St James over the past years. Was anyone aware that tropical fevers not previously known in the region had declared themselves in Grenada, Carriacou and Bequia? Mrs Allard here, she'd succumbed to one of these and not a word had appeared in the press, as far as Ms Baker knew. Would Mr Carr please report this, as well as the employing of poisoned feathers and the defoliation of trees, down at the lagoon in particular, where there was a primal jungle much in need of conservation? Did Mr Carr know that a Mr Jim Davy, who was involved in the local Craft Centre, had put in a large amount of US dollars, as she could stand witness? Didn't all this add up to a concerted effort on the part of the United States of America to 'destabilize' any island with a régime that favoured the people?

Maldwin Carr inclined his head gravely, the white man who was both judged and judge in this outpouring. An expression of infinite tiredness gave him the look of a don listening to the paper of a faintly disliked student. The girl, he noted, was sitting bolt-upright on her rug. Her eyes were filled with tears – she was a fiercely feeling one all right – and he cursed those like Holly or Mr Julian Byrne who were able to play with emotions so cynically. There was a look of astonishment and respect too: Maldwin Carr noted that it was clear, from the girl's expression, that Holly had not spoken in this way on their earlier encounter in the store. And he wondered why that might be.

In London – going to the house, trying to gain admission by the front door, realizing the girl's mother, Teza, was away, going down the basement steps and finding himself let in by a sharp-featured woman who called herself Eleanore – Maldwin Carr had been struck by the girl's quick acceptance of his plan. She would set something off here, there was no doubt. She'd gone out of the room and he'd asked Eleanore, quite casually, whether Mari knew what she was in for, embarking on a probably disappointing quest – and, could he hint at least, very likely with dubious political backing from somewhere or other that might land her in considerable danger? Eleanore had flared up, as he might have guessed she would. Mari had every right to go looking for her father. Did Mr Carr know that in all the years Ford had failed to take an interest in the child her doubts and fears had grown, so she thought in the end she was the most unwanted human being that ever walked the face of the earth? Whatever might happen when she arrived, it was a vital journey for the girl, and if Mr Carr was afraid that things would 'get set off' – she made Mari sound like some automatic combustible squib, which would explode on contact with the island of her origin – then all the more reason to keep a close eye on her. And Lore had gone into the kitchen and come back and said, 'We're right out of wine.'

And Maldwin had bought a bottle at the off-licence and come back, and Mari had gone out with friends, and he had said to the woman as they drank at the kitchen table, 'I do think you could tell me more about Mari's . . . expectations . . . when she arrives in St James. And your friend Holly Baker, do you ever hear from her? Surely she would tell you if Ford had gone out to the island and been involved in some insurrection or other and then been killed? That's what they're thinking in England, you know.'

'But who's "they"?' was all Lore would say in reply.

Now Holly Baker had crossed the room and opened the door of what seemed to be a cupboard but showed in the gloom to be a chipped bath, a shower fixture with a sagging plastic curtain and a cooker. From the cooker she pulled out a bottle of rum. Mugs followed. Maldwin Carr noted that Ms Baker moved with quiet satisfaction, as if preparing a bombshell – in the way of information at least. How many years in London had she missed? Maldwin Carr thought that it was likely Holly Baker had reached a stage in her life where she was ready to believe any of the mixed-up stories she invented for herself.

There was more than a hint of melodrama in the air. Maldwin Carr was aware, as Holly poured the rum and the girl looked up at her from the floor, of being set up as a spectator at a hackneyed but still powerful piece of theatre. 'Yes,' Holly was saying as she poured from a can of flat Coca Cola into the mugs of rum, 'I certainly can remember who was shot on the hill and came down in the sea. Why do you suggest that this feat of memory is beyond me?'

He didn't, of course. Maldwin Carr spoke quickly and nervously to show his acceptance of having been a little too arrogant with Holly Baker, that he was now on her territory, and that he would be happy, furthermore, to accept a warm and positively nauseating drink from her. 'Cuba Libre,' Holly murmured as she sipped at her mug, which was scorched dark brown with a succession of unwashed-up powdered coffees. 'I snitch a bottle of rum from the bar from time to time, when the big boss isn't looking.'

'And who's the big boss?' said Maldwin Carr gently. It

was, as he wrote in his pad at the end of the following day, as if he could feel Holly veering and leaning with the wind, racing in full sail, tacking between truth and fantasy, the longed-for and the true.

'The boss,' said Holly, giving a little dance step as she recrossed the room, but this time to sit on her bed, so Mari had to swivel round to stare up at her like an acolyte at the priestess of some mysterious, under-funded cult. 'The boss is still Sanjay, of course. For a little while longer only, it's true.' Holly looked down derisively at the girl. 'Hey, drink up, you,' she said. 'You gotta get gay for the evening, you go all Christmas, eh?' And she threw back her head and laughed, so Maldwin Carr wondered if Holly Baker had not been drinking all afternoon in the stifling prison of the store. Then again it occurred to him that she might be acting – hamming it up, in fact – to conceal her own deep uncertainty.

On the day Ford came and I went down to the lagoon and I saw Sanjay, that's when I made my mistake. I should have left this damn place then. Now this man sits in my room with a pad on his knee and the poor girl crouches on the floor like she's expecting bad news and she's digging herself into a hole getting ready for it. Of course, I should have seen that meeting when I walked back over the lumpy sand. Those feathers in my path meant Tanty Grace was at work, that she was pushing Sanjay out of the way as if he wasn't worth more than a pile of the bulky-tail shirts she's washed for him all these years. And seeing Mighty Barby running through the trees on my way back, I also saw that our days were suddenly numbered. For Ford must have sent Mighty Barby down to the lagoon with those bags of guns. The guns and the white feathers. St James isn't our home any more. But I didn't know it then. I just walked on up to the old wooden house. Beyond the verandah, door swinging open, stood the decrepit museum of Sanjay's eccentric taste. Pandora had left the verandah and gone to roam around there – it was one of the few places she was allowed because she was quiet in there for hours on end. No doubt the exhibits, with their roots in the realm of ignorance and fantasy – a merman's tail, a thunderstruck hair, an embalmed piglet with a dappled, translucent skin and aquamarines for eyes – no doubt these matched the bizarre assortment of images in her head. And there was no door out the back: Tanty Grace could sit on the verandah with her darning and still look out and see the girl, wandering in her father's strange collection.

That day Pandora had paused by the replica of the Pompeian Slave and his Mistress and was looking up with a kind of innocent longing at the frozen embrace. I went into the museum and came up behind her in silence, so when I said her name she did a jump, and her eyes stared at me like great bowls of blue water while she tried to pull herself back from the act of love she'd never known and could only imagine aloud – in those sad, desperate wailings – with her father. I told Pandora I wanted to take her for a little walk. And Tanty Grace, hearing me from the verandah, nodded her head in sleepy approval. No one can think what to do with Pandora since she's been bombed out of her asylum. Sanjay just stands looking at her with his face stony in grief, frozen like the love-makers, only in tragedy.

'I'll take you down to the creek at the lagoon,' I said to Pandora, although I knew she couldn't understand. She nodded happily and put her hand in mine. If she hadn't been quite a few inches taller than me, it would have been just like the old days, when Dora used to get me to take the child for a walk so she could try to get Sanjay interested in her again on those long, hot afternoons when even her milky blood came to the boil and she began to sway about as if she had a pain up in her arse. Don't forget, Holly, I'd say to myself as I set off with that little gold-and-white cherub down to the beach ('I don't want Millie around, she gets on my nerves,' Dora would say in those days), don't forget the saying, 'Grenada is south of Paradise and north of Frustration.' And I'd think, If this is Paradise, I can't wait for a trip to Frustration. But I took the kid all the same, although I didn't like her, and that feeling was reciprocated, I'm afraid.

Now all is forgotten. The clouds of madness have come down and wiped out the past. I set a straw hat on Pandora's head and went back on the track to the lagoon. The sun – Pandora says sometimes she sees a black sun and that day I almost knew what she meant – came down on us like a burned, frayed egg, and no white around it, in the sky. Pandora's hand soon sweated terribly, but she didn't let go. As we reached the first trees, Mighty Barby darted out towards us, and for a moment I thought how strange it was, a white woman who'd gone out of her mind and an albino Negro who'd been driven mad because he was a freak of nature, meeting on that hot track and turning their eyes from each other, which is what they did. Mighty Barby's eyes were small and red and fringed with wheat-coloured lashes. He was excited and burbling something impossible to understand. If I hadn't had that uneasy feeling of being with two outcasts somehow, and sensing the sadness of it and all that, I'd have tried to make out what Mighty Barby said. I'm one of the few people who can decipher him when I want. And he would've told me he wasn't going down to the southern tip of the island just for the fun of it either. If I'd stopped twice to think, I'd have got him to tell me why he was there. Because, of course, when I came to think of it, he was fetching and carrying for Ford.

How it takes you back, sitting and thinking and drinking here, as if The Heights was the other side of the world from the trouble. The girl – you could call her an invasion of trouble – moves restlessly on the floor and then goes to stand against the window. She looks guilty, terrified – and so she should, I say, like a hornet that's seen its own sting trail after it, under innocent skin. She looks black against the light. She stares at me like Pandora did when she was a little girl, a few days after Ford and Teza went off in the boat, when I went down to find Sanjay again and Millie was sent out to tell me he wasn't there. 'Very well, I'll take Pandora out for a walk,' I said, and I could hear the child's mother moving behind the slatted blinds in the old bedroom that leads out on the verandah.

'Sanjay,' she murmured, 'get that silly fool of a woman out of here for good.' (Dora must have come through the trees after all, I thought then, and seen Sanjay and me together in the house under the palm fronds, with the small lopsided window looking out. She must have stared in at us. And now she was tormenting Sanjay again, threatening him with the ending of her own life and his conscience burdened with that ending for the rest of his.) 'Get that bitch out,' she said as I walked. I remember my feet were heavy and I couldn't pick them up, and I called to little Pandora and took her to the creek where we'd all been so happy picnicking just a short time before. It seemed like years. Teza (practical, knows-what-she-wants Teza) had climbed into a fisherman's boat of all things and gone off with a boy who would become a poet and a political force and a poet and a singer again before changing his name to an African name, and then back again – and then, for what?

'Let's go and see the boats, darling,' I said to little Pandora. I remember, as we passed the mouth of the creek and pushed up through what was still then primary jungle in Sanjay's forgotten and preserved tip of the lagoon, that Pandora tried to pull back. 'Come on,' I said. 'The lovely boats your Daddy made – come and see the boats.'

I really couldn't do anything with the child. As I said

before, it may have been the day at the picnic that had frightened her. How can you tell? She was unbalanced anyway, I think to myself. Well, she was whining before we even got to the little harbour. The water had gone down quite a bit in the last few days. It's these strange tides you get out here, which drain right away from the reef at the edge of the lagoon, and it's at these times the great pots show up, sticking up in the sand like humps under bedclothes.

Now there was an abandoned look about the little port, and the ships stood with the masts half-collapsed – 'In case there's a hurricane,' Sanjay used to say, to frighten the children and make them laugh. There was a bloody great snake drooped over the mud walls the children had built. But I don't honestly think it was this that sent Pandora into such fits of screaming. Oddly enough, what seemed to send her off was the child who wandered about there too – quite absorbed in her game of shifting sand from one pile to another and pushing and pulling Sanjay's model ships at the end of a length of string. It was the child from the village, the child in the pink dress who'd been cheated of her play with the ship before the picnic when Duchess Dora was there, not the snake, which slithered off quickly into the undergrowth. But Pandora had started up, and she wouldn't stop.

I went back to the Bar. As I said, that was the first time those screams came right up the beach and I thought to myself, well, either the child's mother or Millie is going to have to break into the siesta hour now and go and smooth things over. She was jealous, I suppose, poor little half-spoilt, half-neglected thing – and there'd been some tussle on the picnic day at the harbour with the village kids. She wanted Sanjay for herself, which is a silly wish at the best of times. (I have to admit, I sometimes wonder if, on that day of the picnic, she didn't walk along the jungle path with her mother and they both looked in at us. But it's most unlikely, as Dora never took her daughter anywhere.)

'It's too late now to make it up to Pandora,' I said on the day Ford came and I went down to the lagoon to find Sanjay. 'And you know she'll very likely never get well.' But he just shook his head. I looked down at his hands and they were hanging loose – big, sensitive hands – in a way that used to drive me mad with irritation. It was like saying, 'I'm powerless.' He had a thick gold wedding band on his fourth finger. I could have cut it off him after Dora died. He used to sit in the Bar and tap his glass of rum against the gold. And Pandora wears the little gold ring he gave her as a child. It would be sent back from the asylum in Grenada to Sanjay when it grew too small for her, and Sanjay sent it to Barbados to be made bigger, and it was sent back again, and so on. She still wears it now.

'I can't leave the island, I can't leave Pandora,' Sanjay says. And yet he sits with his head bowed on the verandah night after night as Pandora screams for him and Tanty Grace has to give her herb medicines to calm her down.

If it's a question of telling this man, with his smug face and his pre-packed knowledge of women – label 'older woman', label 'moderately attractive', label 'shrew' or 'nag' – then I'll tell him what I want and when I want to. Get your American friends in, darling, I'll say, the revolution is starting. My pal what you met in a basement in London – another recipient of Mother Teza's charity, you might say – tells me in a letter that our girl Mari here will walk to the southern point of the island tonight and shine a light and let the reds in under our beds. Keep ever so strict an eye on her, but she'll still steal away from you like a shadow, leaving just a white husk behind. Or maybe you like that, Mr Stiff Upper Lip Man, with your public school need to conceal and betray. Maybe you're a bloody spy like the rest of them. And you're here to welcome the Austin faction with open arms. Who knows, or cares, for that matter? What difference does it make which pigs get into power and run the world?

It does bring a smile, though, to think of Mari – Marina, that is, the lost darling – walking all unknowing past the wooden house where Sanjay sits and Pandora lies a few feet away, moaning for him. Marina, carrying her revolutionary ideals, her dreams, her love of her vanished father and her ancestry on this cruel island, where her forebears slaved and kept silent under the eye of the old Allards and then, when night fell, danced and sang till sun-up, kings of the imaginings of the night. Let her dreams come true! They've as much chance of that happening as the dreams and stories the slaves had of staying hard and bright when the sun came over the sea to melt them. But that's not right, of course. Her dreams have every chance of coming true now. Her revolutionary heroes will come, dressed up as Fairy Godmother in the carnival. The only trouble is, it's the Fairy Godmother in this case who so often turns into a pumpkin – and, worst of all, a pumpkin that doesn't roll away with the dawn.

Still, there's no need to be cynical about the aims of a young woman like Marina. She comes here to bring in one invasion and she'll trigger off another, in the shape of the biggest pumpkin of the lot, the US of A.

How does it go? I thought of the words the minute I saw that blot on the water, the head swimming in, half-under the sea. The words of a black woman writer, Alice Walker, of her heroine Meridian:

> But at other times her dedication to her promise came back strongly . . . On those occasions such was her rage that she actually felt as if the rich and racist of the world should stand in fear of her, because she – though apparently weak and penniless, a little crazy and without power – was yet of resolute and fearless character, which, sufficient in its calm acceptance of its own purpose, could bring the mightiest country to its knees.

You can see it all in her eyes. They shine with her knowledge that she is the future. She is the light. She, with her calm acceptance of purpose, can bring the mightiest country to its knees. God help us all.

'Marina,' I say. She looks startled: she doesn't know I know her full name and what she tells to Lore – already now she begins to suspect I know her plans. Her eyes stare quite insolently at me, as if she couldn't care less whether or not I tell her the one thing she wants most in the world to know. Or does it matter to her less than I think? Whether Ford is dead or not? Has the ideal taken over from reality? Will she be as proud and as happy to give him an honourable burial – attended, no doubt, by black Marxist-Leninist troops who will stand round the grave with their gun salute – as to greet him with open arms? I'd rather not try to answer that. That's something I don't want to know.

'If you . . . come across a strange-seeming kind of girl,' I say, 'when you go down to the lagoon . . .' And my voice tails off. I don't like to say 'white'. 'Her name is Pandora. Be careful with her a little, she isn't well.'

Maldwin Carr's pencil starts to race. What good this will do him I couldn't say. But I think to myself that it's a world created by the Mr Carrs that's ultimately responsible for a girl like Pandora going mad. No calm acceptance of purpose for her – no purpose at all, more likely. She fell under the hand of a man, her father in this case, but a rich man a powerful, white casual man, and she fell to pieces because of it.

But Marina has her purpose – and it may be better to kill and burn than to incinerate yourself. Marina may seem 'a little crazy', like Meridian in Alice Walker's book, but she's not crazy, to her own mind, like Pandora.

And thinking all this, I dare say that's when I made my first decision. Just to teach you, Marina, that your pure-little-revolutionary act can be pretty irritating to an old cynic like me. These things can jump two ways, you know. You come to find your roots on the magical island of St James, baby. OK, so I'll help you with your identity. And maybe you and that poor mad girl will have something to cry about together after all.

'This girl Pandora may say strange things,' I say into Marina's cool, intent eyes, 'but she doesn't know what she says.' And as Marina frowns, puzzling out what I can possibly mean, I say under my breath to Pandora how sorry I am. 'But I just had to get you away from here. You won't get better anyway . . . and you do need looking after properly, you know. I just had to do what I did, and you don't know – you can't remember – at the best of times.'

Maurice Bishop, Prime Minister of Grenada, was murdered on 19 October 1983. He and his girlfriend, Education Minister, Jacqueline Creft, were freed from house arrest by an adoring crowd of fellow Grenadians. The prisoners were confused and a little stiff: they'd been tied for some days to iron bedsteads. All the same, they made a triumphant re-entry to St George's. They were very hungry and Mrs Creft, Jackie's mother, rushed out as the procession passed her door and said, 'Hold it, I'll bring you out some bread.' But by the time she'd run into the kitchen and back out again, the procession had surged on. She never saw her daughter again. I don't know why – that story seems to me the saddest one of all. And yet Ford's belief in a pure Leninist state for the little West Indian island went quite undiminished. Maybe he's right, who knows? They gunned down Bishop and his men, and Bishop's last words were, 'Oh God, oh God, they turned their guns against the masses!'

On 27 October US marines arrived at St George's. Hudson Austin and Bernard Coard, leaders of the coup, were arrested. The Grenadians were delighted to welcome American troops.

I thought about these things just after the coup, two months ago, when I took Pandora's big limp hand and we walked down to the lagoon again, turning this time up to the creek. Maybe Ford is right. There's no place in the world any more for people like Sanjay, or his expensively crazy daughter, or his houses, or his books rotting in an old library with tropical fern growing through the roof, or for me, for that matter. But I'm just one who didn't get away.

'They'll never let you leave the island without a generous handshake,' Lore wrote. 'All those years of hard work you've put in on St James. All that standing in the store till your legs drop off.'

Ha, Lore, if only you knew. Last time I was trying to get my act together and move off of this place, I asked Jim Davy to ask Sanjay and the consortium what my redundancy would be – tactful, if you know what I mean. No, I wrote to Lore, Jim Davy came back to me saying they'd give a real good party in the Bar with fireworks and the lot. And he said with that creepy little smile of his, 'And Sanjay'll have a gold bracelet for you, I've no doubt. Something of Dora's – that poor daughter can't want her mother's jewellery.'

Oh thank you, Mr Davy, I sure am glad I asked. 'As for the girl,' I said to Jim Davy, 'you'll really have to take her off the island. She'll put off overseas investment. She was naked at the north point the other day, you know, trying to fuck a palm tree down by the edge of the water. Mighty Barby was on the beach, laughing. A whole party of Japanese businessmen touring the island in the consortium's antique sloop turned back out to sea so as not to have to witness it.'

Pandora's much worse now – and I was thinking all the time we were walking to the creek that day how to make her worse, so Jim Davy would come and take her away.

As it turned out, it was all much easier than I'd expected. The big digger and dumper owned by the Venezuelans on the island had cut a swathe right through the jungle, and just where the little harbour used to be, grown over now for ever so many years since the last time I took the silly kid there and she screamed her head off at her precious ships played with by somebody else. 'You have to share in life, don't you, Pandora?' I said as we turned up the creek and stood staring a moment at the red gash in the earth made by the digger, the tyre marks like giant fish scales on the drying track. Beyond, stale water glinted yellow in the new clearing under the trees.

'Sharing is called democracy,' I said to the poor idiotic girl and she laughed at me with her thin lips. She seemed happy and quite excited. 'Or it's called socialism,' I said, and at that moment I decided Ford was right. I pushed Pandora gently ahead of me until she reached the edge of the harbour and the first skeletal masts of her father's model ships peered blackly up at her through a cloud of steam on the water. I thought too of Dora at this moment – I don't know why – dancing in the Rose Drawing Room of her freezing mansion in West Cork. Her eyes were bright. She wore a whole row of bracelets, and they slipped and crashed like coins at a gaming table.

'Look what we have here!' I said to Pandora, as if we'd stumbled on the Wizard of Oz at a birthday treat. I knelt down, pulling her with me to the edge of the greenish-black slime that now filled the toy marina. The ships must have been preserved by it being so windless and airless here. 'Now just fancy that!' And I began to pull at the tattered sails. A boom, fragile as a mummified finger, crashed without sound into the ooze.

'No!' Pandora cried. 'No! No! No!'

I won't go on here about the ensuing scene. What memories came into the girl's splintered mind I'd find hard to say. There was Daddy, of course . . . and marina . . . and marina again . . . and Millie and dress, pink dress, something like that. Poor Pandora, the mosaic nearly fitted. Then it blew to smithereens again.

But when she's safely gone with Jim Davy – and to be properly cared for, this time – I'll make sure Sanjay looks around at this Godforsaken island and finds nothing to keep him on it at all.

So that must have been when I made my decision. I stopped at Millie's on my way back to The Heights. She was in her yard and she came out with that slow, very serious look of hers that she wears sometimes just to stop the guests at Carib's Rest from patronizing her, expecting a bright white smile in a friendly face along with the fancy grouper fish she's been taught to cook with a sauce of fresh lime and walnut chopped up. But I saw she'd been thinking more deeply than that. So have I, Millie, I said to myself, before saying quite casually, 'By the way, Ford blew in this afternoon. Can you beat it? After all these years.'

It was clear Millie'd already seen him because she just went on nodding, as if I'd said nothing of interest at all. I felt all at once then that I'll miss Millie when Sanjay and I leave the island – I'll even miss Tanty Grace, who looks at me so kindly and forgivingly, even though she knows the secret of the terrible thing I wished, and which she brought about, whatever anyone may say about this biological warfare stuff. I'll miss Tanty Grace for finding evil natural and so making it possible to live in a place like this, where everything is so beautiful but there's just no hope. It's hard too to imagine Millie and Tanty Grace going on living here when I'm gone – as if they come to life only when I look at them. Of course, with Sanjay gone too they'll have to do other things – go and get jobs with the Venezuelans, go up to the States maybe . . .

'He say he come back an see me again tonight. It is folks who coming to see he. And I say they come here when . . .'

Millie's words, like my thoughts, tailed off. How much does she know? I wondered. But why should she take a risk?

Poor Millie, all she's done is obey orders. First Sanjay ('Wash my shirts'), then Mrs Van der Pyck ('Cook this way and that way'), then Ford, back after all this time to tell her what she wants in life after all. Then I remembered that Ford was right. You had to tell people what to want in this kind of a situation. The whole thing stuck in my throat rather all the same. And the danger was quite taken for granted. What the hell happens, I thought (for I was afraid to say it to Millie), if US marines land here tonight too and Millie gets killed in the crossfire? Just like what harm did Millie ever do anyone? And my eyes filled with tears, thinking of Jackie Creft's mother and the loaf of bread she went quickly – but it was impossible to be quick enough – into the kitchen to get. All Millie has done is feed people, care for people. Such reckless loyalty demanded before she's even had a chance of a better life.

'Tell them to come to The Heights,' I said.

Millie looked down the road to where a child was swinging on the branch of a tree. She looked as if she was in two minds whether to go down there and tell the child to stop before the branch broke. And then decided against it. She shook her head. 'He come here,' she said.

And we parted ways, but not before Millie told me she'd bring them after all to my room at The Heights later. I felt like Teza (I can own up to it) that evening, with an important meeting ahead, and maybe violence, or police interference at least. I drank up some rum, but there was plenty left there for the landing. And I thought of them all coming ashore. On to sand and the roots of Sanjay's gnarled, fairytale trees at the southernmost tip of the island.

Later Maldwin Carr would find it hard to say what exactly had led up to Holly's statement. The woman was rambling quite a lot. At one point she even went and pulled down a book from the shelf behind his head and read aloud to him out of it. As he made his notes her voice, thickened with rum, declaimed, 'Your future is the future of Great Britain' and, as he scribbled down his findings on the Ford affair, 'The future of Great Britain is your future.' He knew all this was to impress the girl Mari, who stood by the door like an uncertain soldier, one moment brave and defiant, the next drooping. And impress her all these words did. She never took her eyes off Holly Baker. Maldwin Carr even began to wish he'd never contemplated bringing the girl out to St James with him. But he suppressed the wish, as he was well trained to do in his frequent travels through countries where suffering and deprivation were so great that to feel pity rather than gather news would have been like jumping into the sea with an umbrella. He wrote, glancing up now and again:

> I feel pretty convinced that something is planned for tonight. Both women are very jumpy and there have been no references to Christmas festivities, etc.
>
> Question: how to track down Jim Davy without arousing suspicion? Essential not to let the girl out of sight. A visit to Sanjay Allard not advisable at present. If the girl comes too, she's in such an excitable state I don't doubt she'd let fly at Allard with various wild accusations. Go back to Carib's Rest – get that Van der Pyck woman to hold Mari while I pop down to the south of the island and see Allard before dinner. Not safe, she'll be too tied up with her preparations. Leave in ten minutes if nothing more emanating from Baker.

As Maldwin Carr sat and scribbled, his mind went back to the parties where he'd seen Dora and Sanjay – the spontaneous and glorious sixties parties, where Jimi Hendrix played and Janis Joplin and the spirit of self-love dressed up to let it all hang out went in a camp-fire throb and wail. And excitement was so great that the girls seemed to grow and expand as the party wore on, like the Japanese paper flowers that you put in water. How Sanjay had loved paying for them! For the men in Mr Fish shirts too, and all the dope, and another room for boozing. How glad he'd been to greet his friends: hip publishers; young film directors trying to capture on film those already superannuated giants, Sonny Rollins, Thelonius Monk, John Coltrane; women who worked on fashion magazines and looked anything but – more like mermaids captured in an aquarium, long hair and faces ghastly with too many late nights. And Maldwin among them – 'My favourite spy!' and Sanjay was holding out his arms in that laughing, slightly self-deprecating way. No one had expected Sanjay (no one who knew him at school, that is) to make such a pile of money. But his easily disposable, amusing ideas were just right for the times. Maldwin bit back a smile, remembering the craze for 'instant' paper clothes, and Sanjay's brightly coloured cheap little cameras which took twenty photographs and then you threw them away, like a briquet lighter. 'After all, who wants more than twenty photographs?' Sanjay would say. 'They're so boring.'

The party Maldwin remembered hadn't been more than a stone's throw from where this girl's mother, Teza, lived now. As well as the girls with legs like cricket bats sticking out of mini skirts and men who, with their long hair, looked like portraits of Renaissance crooks, there were one or two black men, as Maldwin remembered – and one black woman who was a lawyer and had been brought along and stood laughing at the dissipation of the scene, and a Sudanese who ran an 'alternative' magazine, and an Indian recently acclaimed as the best prose writer of his generation. Things were different now – there was no free and happy atmosphere any more. After the gloom and destruction of the last sixteen years, it was little wonder. Maldwin pulled himself back to the present and thought, with what was almost a pang, that

Mari would hardly have been born at the time of that party.

He rose. An elegant wrist shot out from a cuff to show the marking of time, the hour of dinner at the hotel. He cleared his throat, a further signal to the girl who stood now completely entranced by Holly, as if she had herself been the author of all these wise and true words and would save the world for Mari if she wanted it. 'Mari, my dear, we should go,' said Maldwin Carr gently. 'We shall see Holly again after dinner, no doubt.' And he turned to Holly with a small, gallant smile, as if they were all in the foyer of a London theatre and not on a small island on the brink of terrible trouble.

'My father . . .' Mari said. Her cheeks were burning. She looked quite lovely, Maldwin thought. It was a pity for a girl like that to involve herself in something as unrewarding as revolutionary politics.

'Your father is here,' Holly said.

There was a silence. Then, 'So . . . did you . . . you . . . save him?' Mari's words came very faint, more of a statement than a question. For the first time she lowered her eyes, as if the news was too much to bear in the presence of others.

'I hope to,' Holly said.

'He's – he's here?'

'Yes, you'll find him,' Holly said, 'on the island.'

NIGHT

Lanterns had been lit up on the verandah of Carib's Rest by the time Maldwin Carr and his companion, a mountain-honey-coloured girl who attracted a good many glances from early merrymakers, had come over in the jeep from The Heights and parked in the grassy lot screened off by hibiscus bushes. The decorations, like those in the Bar, had that amateurish, nursery look that Maldwin could identify immediately with an English upper-class childhood. The hand of Sanjay was here still, however much the consortium might introduce teak bars and air conditioning and 'local' specialities that tasted of almost nothing, in their frangipani frills and pools of piquant sauce. There were half-broken paper lanterns and streamers, forgotten or overlooked, presumably, by the smart interior decorator from New York and coming out once a year when it was too late to do anything to change them. Maldwin Carr smiled. He wondered that Mrs Van der Pyck was ready to wreck her luxurious hotel, in appearance at least, and to transform it to a youth club hall or some such – and Mari, of course, was quite unsurprised by it. 'Now you'll go to the cottage and get ready,' Maldwin said, for he was afraid that the girl who was walking beside him like a zombie might turn on her heel and fly away. But he needn't have worried after all. She followed him quite passively to the row of gingerbread cottages that had once housed the slaves of the Allard estate. Ten minutes after she'd gone in, she was out again, silent as ever, her only concession to 'getting ready', as far as Maldwin Carr could see, being a cosmetic one.

'Heads would turn all right,' as Maldwin told his audience when the night was over, and a succession of nights after that, and he was safely back home. You didn't often see anything like Mari – at least he hadn't, and it was clear that the visitors to Carib's Rest on Christmas Eve hadn't either. It was the strangest thing. Mari's face white as a mime. Great eyes circled in black. A mouth so red it looked like a flamboyant. And all the flowers seemed to crowd in now that night had really begun: Maldwin saw them in the dip of light from the floodlights, below the cottonhouse steps and creeping along the railings of the verandah. Hibiscus and flamboyant gaping and pushing out at them as he and the girl walked to their table. A general silence fell. In the white dip of light he saw the flowers on the paw-paw tree, and the flowers on the soursop tree, and the flowers on the mango tree, and the flowers on the guava tree, and the lilies planted for guests to look out at to interrupt the uninterrupted view of the sea, all grow big and stretch out towards them as they went. It was quite unnerving, Maldwin said, something to do with the weird state the girl was in – and it brought it home to him again that tropical nights were something you forgot quickly when you were away from them, but when you returned and they came down on you, you remembered that uneasy feeling all right. The girl Mari could well have been one of those soucriants, he said, the spirits that like to dress up as beautiful women and stare out at you from the trees at night with their big eyes. It was like following something like that – and he was glad, absurdly so to tell the truth, when they reached their table.

The girl had spoken once on the way down the verandah, where the ever-blowing trade wind brought in the thick scents from the flowers on the trees and mixed them with the women diners' French perfume. Mrs Van der Pyck, all sapphire blue eyes and red hair – nervous, Maldwin could see, at the appearance of this strange young woman and the possible repercussions on the guests – was foolish enough to step into the girl's path. Not for the first time Maldwin Carr wished that convention and his English public-school upbringing did not force him to walk behind a lady when going in to dinner.

But it was too late. Mrs Van der Pyck stood and smiled an inane smile into the face of this girl whose face was like a white bell flower.

'I put some lovely irises on your table' – some such nonsense. And then, 'I do hope, Mr Carr and er . . . Miss . . . that you'll find everything just as you want tonight.'

'What we want,' said Marina – and Maldwin reported that you could have cut the silence at that moment with a knife – 'what we want, madam, is a Revolution.' And she swept on to pull out her chair and sit down before Maldwin Carr could do the proper thing and help her.

It seemed interminable, he said, the time it took for a buzz of conversation to start up. But then, as in a film, a glass did fall and break on the wooden floor and a high laugh turned the atmosphere jovial, if rather frenetic. And Mrs Van der Pyck went as fast as her stiletto heels would carry her to put on Frank Sinatra on the cassette player in the long, panelled room.

'Things didn't change much, even then,' Maldwin said later, as he made the wry face for which he was well known among friends and foreign correspondents, at his club. Any trouble in these far-flung spots and the gringos will relax to the sound of Ol' Blue Eyes. But somehow, tonight, Maldwin had the feeling these comforting strains wouldn't be quite enough.

The effect on the diners of Mari's reply to their hostess's polite concern for her welfare – well, it was as if a sudden feverish sleep had fallen on the guests on the verandah at Carib's Rest. Not a single person there woke or looked ordinarily about until the first bars of the Sinatra tape went on.

When Sanjay arrived the party on the verandah relaxed, and Mrs Van der Pyck doled out Christmas punch, and all the lights were turned off, which left only candles in glass holders flickering on each table. To walk meant brushing against the paper streamers, invisible now, and some of the women, as they moved from table to table, gave low cries like birds at the touch, as if walking in a wood in a dream. A pudding came in, held aloft by Millie and flaming merrily. Mistletoe, fresh from polythene and a flight from London to Barbados, was tied in bunches and was then there apparently by magic in the rafters over the verandah, the dark wire hidden in the tropical blackness.

Out beyond the balustrade a full moon hung with the same insouciance over lawn, coconut palms and the sea. Maldwin Carr, with a table as near to the steps as he could get, looked out at it – and back at Sanjay, not very different after all these years after all – as he smiled at the guests and allowed his back to be thumped with good Christmas will. Wasn't the poor bloke about to surrender his lease? Maldwin remembered and felt a surge of pity for him. What the hell *did* a man like Sanjay do when he'd reached the end of his resources, emotional and financial, as Sanjay obviously had? Stay and watch his old house done up, like this one, as a club for winter visitors? Stay on as steward or overseer? It seemed unthinkable somehow. At the same time Maldwin was aware that pity for Sanjay was not strictly necessary. Even if there was something childlike and untouched about the man, that made you sorry for him. It was when you thought of him up against it in a tough modern world. All of which was pure sentimentality, of course. It was partly to do with the rearing – and the schooling they'd both had too. You could see Sanjay walking across his fields or moors with the absolute confidence that belongs to those who have been brought up to believe that ownership of the land goes with the Act of Creation, that the Lord gave to the local landlord as if by some mysterious right. There was the dignified, bow-windowed library, where all the books, written by the world's greatest writers, also belonged to you. You owned the writers, too. There was the smell of the walnut desk, and the old leather cigar box, and a bowl of dried rose petals, the roses picked by a great-aunt as she went stiffly with her dress hitched up and her bustle bobbing like a rabbit's tail among the bushes in the garden. The bowl, blue-and-white Chinese – Maldwin saw the scene and smelt the scene and saw the sides of the earth, East and West, welded together to serve the afternoon tea in the library of Sanjay's forebears. So why feel for him now? Sanjay had a very sweet smile, of course, and there were at least three women hanging over him at any given time: 'Sanjay, you're such a recluse!' 'Sanjay, won't you come to Mégève with us for the New Year?' But it wasn't this that made Maldwin feel a little for Sanjay that night. It was, perhaps, that Sanjay was the last imprint of a vanishing breed – and he seemed oddly vulnerable, Maldwin thought, as if he might shortly vanish himself. But maybe these apprehensions were the result of having the girl with him on this island that looked so placid out there under the moon.

Maldwin was too busy with his thoughts – not that that was how he'd put it later, when asked to account for the girl's disappearance. He'd say instead that it was an American who distracted him – he said his name was Jim Davy and he held out an arm and a hand as scaly as a tortoise's. They were both wearing paper hats; the stage had been reached of crackers and riddles and jokes, while the St Jamesian boys stood in the doorway to the long room looking out on the verandah in grave amazement at the winter visitors' idea of merriment. Maldwin could say he'd turned back from looking out at the preposterously big moon, hanging there and lighting up the corrugated iron roof of Holly's store below like the outline of an evil cottage in a children's book. And when he turned back the girl had slipped away.

In fact, Maldwin had seen Sanjay begin to notice Mari's extraordinary beauty, grotesquely and clownishly made up though she was. As the American and Venezuelan women hung on him and Mrs Van der Pyck came up, ever-hopeful, with a bottle of Armagnac and an assortment of stockings packed with gifts that she would throw wildly among the tables, he saw Sanjay look out at the moon and in again at the other face of whiteness sitting by a candle at the far table where all the flowers came in. Maldwin saw him rise, gently shake off his admirers, as if they too were clinging vines or clematis, and make his way over to her. He saw Sanjay recognize him when he was halfway there – but Sanjay was too dazed, too struck by Mari, to turn back now.

'Sanjay! Where are you going? Are we going to dance?' came the voices of the women, and hands coiled round his neck, pulled at his hair, hooked through his arm. 'Shall we go to the Bar?' 'That would be fun!' 'See if Ferdie's got a new punch for us like Christmas last year!'

Sanjay and Maldwin exchanged greetings. 'And what brings you out to St James?' Sanjay said, but not in the words he would normally use and without taking his eyes off the strange girl sitting at Maldwin Carr's table, with her eyes now on Sanjay. Her eyes floated like waterlilies in a pool fenced with barbed wire. Maldwin saw that Sanjay had never seen eyes like that before. And, set in the made-up white face as they were, they seemed to be blazing with hostility. Sanjay stared. Music came loud from the long room. In an effort to persuade the guests to stay at the hotel, to put off the drunken Christmas Eve wander down to the Bar, Mrs Van der Pyck had put on a tape of early rock 'n' roll.

Sanjay held out his hand. 'Come and dance,' he said to the girl. And Maldwin, who knew he should have found some reason for forbidding it, let her go.

I had to go back to the store. I waited until they'd gone – the man who was playing 007 and the girl who may say she wants an extreme left-wing revolution but is more likely, by the looks of her, to end up as a *Playboy* centrefold. I walked from The Heights to the village, and a boy there who is a cousin of Ford's was sitting on a little motorbike thing, and he gave me a lift down to the store. I have to get the spade, you see, I nearly told him. But in the end I kept my mouth shut. Bring 'em all in and the blaze could go anywhere. I have to get the spade and go to the southern tip of the island, past the red new earth where the diggers and dumpers went in.

I nipped in to the Bar first for a quick one. There weren't too many customers there, when you consider it was Christmas Eve – only the bores, who don't manage to get a table at Carib's Rest, and the engineers working for the consortium on constructing houses and pipe laying and the rest, who aren't considered high-class enough. One of the bores, a fifty-ish man with a small house up in the north, near the old Allard place, pulled at my arm. The jukebox was playing 'I'm Dreaming of a White Christmas' while Ferdie giggled behind the bar.

I could see the fun under way at Carib's Rest by going out to the end of the bar-raft and looking up. There are the scissor palms and a bloody great moon that certainly ought to help things along tonight, and people in posh dresses wandering about on the verandah of the hotel. I thought, I'll very likely see that girl next, she's doubtless half-fallen in love with the whole way of life already. And I saw the people like cut-outs, those cardboard figures you shoot down at a fair. I wonder how many of them will still be around after tonight.

'And how's our lovely female brigand?' said the bore.

And, 'Oh yes, that's me,' I said.

'Sail the seven seas, eh, Holly?'

'Yeah, pick up me cutlass an go.' But tonight, as Ferdie made his usual joke about my credit running out and Bing

Crosby drooled over a sea that's flat and pearly under the moon and lying out there like a stomach with stretch marks, I felt only a terrible weary feeling and tense as a snapping wire as well. 'Another rum and Coke, a Cuba Libre, heh?'

I don't know how long I was asleep. I must've crawled down the side of the raft dance floor place on to the sand – to get away from the wandering fingers of the bore, I daresay. I was asleep and I dreamed of Dora in her beautiful house in the West of Ireland, and the horses ready for the hunt, and then the whole lot of them galloping into the sea, which turned from grey and cold to a blue that was so blue and warm that it hurt. I dreamed of Ford. In the old days, the days of Teza's early letters, when she said, 'He's dedicated his new book of poems to you, Holly.' Oh, yes, I said to myself when I thought I'd write back to her, 'Am I a singin' she-dog then?' For that was the name of the long poem that made him famous. 'No, you're London, the spirit of London,' Teza said in the dream. 'Ford likes you. We're happy.' Then they weren't happy any more. In my dream Ford left Teza. I watched in the corner, crouched on stone paws. Like it was one of the lions in Trafalgar Square, but when I looked down it was me – I'd turned to stone and I was crouching there on my chipped stone paws. A singin' she-dog, and on the corner of Portobello Road – where I watched Ford walk away for good, leaving Teza alone in the street and holding a baby. Then Dora came down the market, but even in the dream I knew that was ridiculous and I couldn't help laughing. It must've come out as a kind of snort, so I woke myself, because I came to for a moment and saw the sand just as bright under the moon and a palm cracking and flapping above me like a big bird. And waves – the wind was beginning to get up.

So I just can't tell how long I lay there, with sometimes the beach under me turning to hard London street and me a has-been, a derelict, sleeping rough under a bridge or in a park. I knew I had to go to the store and get the spade – and I did, time and again in the dream – and set off to the far end of the island. Sometimes I passed Sanjay sitting alone on his verandah or standing deep in thought in that crazy museum of his, staring up at the Slave and his Mistress, the plaster all stripey black and white from the moon making shadows as it came in. Sometimes I didn't get as far as that, and was stopped by Millie and Tanty Grace on the road. 'Don't do it,' Tanty Grace said. She was enormous and her shadow lay right along the road like a barrier you couldn't dare to cross. The shadow of her head ended in a sort of blaze, like a witch's fire with black twigs sticking out, and I was frightened of that in the dream and shrank away from her. Millie wasn't smiling for once; she looked quite stern. 'There's been enough trouble caused by you,' Tanty Grace said. 'Leave us all alone.' And then it was suddenly day, much too bright, and a red parakeet, one of the flock Sanjay brought in from Australia, flew down the road and landed right by us. 'Look at those feathers,' Tanty Grace said, and I woke. But the tail feathers were poisoned and I knew somehow in the dream that Dora had put the feathers in her hair at a ball in her house by the grey sea in Ireland and they had clawed into her as she danced, so she fell down dead.

I woke and went along the beach towards the store. My legs ached badly, so I knew I wasn't in the dream any more, and the shape of the shadows was different too, so it must have been quite a lot later. In spite of the waves, and the wind making the palms creak like a bed with a rotten sleeper in it, you could hear the music up at Carib's Rest. Reels, no less! I had to laugh. Then I realized the Bar must be in silence, or the Scotch skirling would've been drowned out by the jukebox. What happened to the drinkers, then? Did they bore themselves into an early night? Surely Ferdie, just to amuse himself, would be listening to reggae, shaking the twenties shaker Dora brought out to the island with her, jumping tracks to the Stones. But it was dead quiet and there weren't even lights – or so I realized when I got my wits together. No lights streaming out over the sea. Something's happening, I thought. And then I knew I wasn't ready for it at all. My stomach turned to a hard lump and my throat went as dry as sand.

Maldwin Carr and Jim Davy sipped brandies on the verandah of Carib's Rest. The girl Marina danced with Sanjay in the long room, and she flashed every few seconds past the open door at the speed of a subliminal image, distracting the journalist but at the same time reassuring him of her presence. Maldwin Carr wouldn't be able to say, later, just when he'd stopped seeing that body go back and forth like a shutter in a camera or like a rapid succession of shots: a white face, moon-shaped, impassive, and black hair spiralling out. It was within a few seconds of Jim Davy's remark, no doubt – and perhaps it was when, hardly able to believe his ears, Maldwin leaned forward to set down the balloon-glass of brandy on the table. He complained that the stem of the glass was sticky, and he took out a pristine linen handkerchief from the breast pocket of his dinner jacket. Maldwin Carr knew very well how to disguise his reactions in this way, yet he did wonder, as he glanced in the near-dark at the anonymous features of the American, whether Mr Davy was quite taken in after all.

'Most certainly Ford is dead,' were the words that had caused Maldwin to set down his glass as casually as possible on the glass table. 'One of my men shot him. Self-defence, I may say.'

'Ah,' said Maldwin.

'Found him walking along with that crazy albino boy and a couple of mailbags. In broad daylight, too. Mailbags full of arms. Makes you wonder if the guy didn't ask for it in some way or another.'

'He was made to open the mailbags by one of your men?' Maldwin said. 'You have a police presence on St James, then?'

At the same time, looking up at the door to the long room and smelling a sudden gust of jasmine blown in from the garden by the rising wind, he saw Mari dance by and he heard himself – to his own surprise, for he wasn't even particularly fond of the girl – let out a sharp sigh. This the wind and the sound of the Scottish reels obliterated, and Mr Davy went on: 'Yes, since the time of the uprising on Grenada. And this was – just a fortnight or so later. A few men – in case of invasion, or arms smuggling . . .' Jim Davy's voice died away, as the reel came to an end. Mrs Van der Pyck's voice, loud and drunk, billowed out from the long room like a mynah bird.

'Why was the death not reported?' Maldwin Carr said. 'You realize there is still uncertainty as to the whereabouts of Ford? Surely, all deaths are on the record?' And Maldwin Carr thought of the millions of unknown and unreported dead in the world, in drought and famine and genocide.

'I don't know about that,' Jim Davy said. 'I do know our man was threatened at gunpoint by Ford when an order was issued for the mailbags to be opened. It so happened another marine who was patrolling the road down to the southern tip of the island came on the scene in that split second. And Ford, well, he jumped in the air and kind of half-ran, half-fell down the hill and into the sea!'

'Ah,' said Maldwin Carr again. He rose suddenly.

'Mr Carr,' Jim Davy said, rising also. 'I was told by Washington that you would supply me with certain information. Am I correct in thinking that you expect some form of invasion this evening?'

'You are,' said Maldwin Carr, who had by this time reached the door to the long room and was gazing in. The reels had stopped and 'White Christmas' was on loud and sickly, drowning even Mrs Van der Pyck as she shouted her season's greetings to the dancers on the darkened floor.

'But I'd like you to tell me one more thing,' Maldwin Carr said in a half-whisper aimed directly at Mr Jim Davy's ear. 'Who told you in the first place that Ford was on the island?'

'Why do you ask me that?' said Jim Davy, as Maldwin's eyes narrowed, and the absence of Mari impressed itself more and more on a room of entwined couples and Sanjay's cheap lanterns tossing back and forth in the wind.

'Because I don't believe Ford's arrival on the island was previously unknown to you – or to your head office,' Maldwin Carr said, still in that soft voice which seemed to have the ability to carry so much more successfully than Mrs Van der Pyck's. 'I believe orders were given to shoot a man fitting Ford's description, and he was in all likelihood not armed – on his person, that is – at all.'

Jim Davy shrugged and Maldwin caught the first intimations of the man's importance and his awareness of it. 'I certainly am not prepared to argue that point,' Jim Davy said. 'We did receive information that Ford had come over to St James. It was our business, also, at that time to collect as much intelligence and conduct as many searches as we saw fit.'

'Indeed,' said Maldwin Carr softly. 'And you used for your information – ?'

'You wouldn't have met her,' Jim Davy said. 'Woman who runs the little store here. Holly Baker by name.'

Envy, rage, like *baligey*, shooting up like the wild banana fronds I stumble through in that jungle they go and cut down. Outside, outside the walls of Thebes where Ford say the singin' she-dog live, I squat on stone paws answering that riddle where the answer is always incest, ruin, death. Red cocoa fruit, golden apple, mango, peach-ripe nutmeg, fruits of paradise inside the walls where the white man lay down his straight paths and keep me out. I should have known. But I walk into things ('That's you, Holly,' they say. 'You a brave girl all right'), and I pick up me cutlass an go.

I carried the spade down the road to the south of the island. The moon was just about big enough to explode and its rays hung down on the place like lines of dirty washing. I turned past the crumbling barn where the slave is sealed for ever in his fake love for his mistress. The door was swinging open, but I didn't look in. Maybe I knew, or guessed. I walked on. Good, dogged Holly. You'll beat that girl to the point tonight although you drank and slept, that's how I muttered to myself as I went, to kill the fear of the jungle with all the sighings that come out of the bushes and the big white flowers like eyes. Good Holly, go and dig up the guns and give them over. You remember what that boy on Grenada say when the gringos come. 'Before the revolution we were not in the light,' he said. 'I rather they kill me dead than I go work for them if they come to take over we land and try to oppress we again.' And all of twelve years old. Right. You're right there, son. I'm bringing you light. And I pushed on past roots in the earth that looked like the heads of prehistoric monsters.

Maybe I knew all along just what it was I would see as I half-fell against an upturned tree that was like a great wheel, with all the spokes mangled and forcing themselves out.

Sanjay held her down. Her face was smothered in white but the stuff was smudging off on one side. She was struggling sometimes, then sometimes she was still, like a winged bird.

You can't tell me I have to say if it is rape. I'll say nothing now but a scream did come out of me.

Maldwin Carr scissored himself into the Carib's Rest jeep, let off the handbrake and went in a cloud of dust that danced about for a bit in the rays of the moon. He'd hardly had a chance to see the woman on the steps of the old cottonhouse – except to note, while at the same time keeping a close eye on Jim Davy at his side, that she had not been at the evening's festivities. He would remember her later – thin face, corn-coloured hair pulled back. And would wish that he had stopped then and that he'd pulled her into the jeep with him, to guide him through the ensuing hours. He saw too, as they went by the Coconut Bar, that it was silent, dark. Silent Night, he thought suddenly. Moves have been made already for a landing. And he felt a surge of loathing for the violence that would come with Christmas. Then the feeling passed as soon as they swung down the narrow road and Jim Davy pointed out the right fork, down to the Allard house. Maldwin Carr had other things than shock or compassion on his mind. He had been in many similar situations all over the world. They produced their own adrenalin, the imminent arrival of violence and the spilling of blood.

The Allard house had all the lights on, yet it felt empty from the moment Maldwin and Jim Davy arrived. Doorways stood open, bead curtains moved like armies of ants in the strong wind, which grew stronger every minute from the sea. A bamboo rocking-chair, pushed right out to the edge of the verandah, creaked back and forth in the currents of air. A bird – one of Sanjay's flock perhaps, released to fly away from the dangers of the neighbouring island and returning in a confusion of obedience to the lagoon, gave piercing cries from a tree in the garden. The jungle, cut by the new machinery, showed the red mouth of the new track and then darkness, where lights from the house failed to penetrate.

As they waited, Maldwin and Jim Davy stood out on the verandah. It was like, Maldwin recounted later, waiting for a time bomb to go off when you've watched the other man set it. (Others commented, after the event, that Maldwin Carr was evidently losing his grip. He has still the weird propensity of being in a trouble spot at the moment of trouble. But on this occasion he clearly had no idea at all of the way the trouble would go.) For Jim Davy, after calling for Mr Allard and failing to get any answer, produced his radio-transmitter and began to transmit. The sudden disappearance of the girl (and Maldwin's concern, of course, that she should have got away) had been a final proof to him of tonight's prospective invasion. Troops must come in.

Every single thing got its other side. And I can do that double thinkin' too. I'm not surprised when they tell me, 'You know who fix this revolution in Grenada? The fuckin' CIA, that's who.' It was practice time in Vieques years before poor old Bishop overthrow an his girl's mother come out too late into the street with bread. The Yanks bomb a Puerto Rican island, Vieques. Ferdie tell me that down at the bar. He say its because they practise for Grenada. Whichever one way you go, the path lead back to the same place.

By the same token, I wasn't surprised to see the girl wandering down to the point just a while after I got there. You may think it romantic-sounding to dig in fine sand by moonlight, but it ain't. I kept stubbing my toes on those bits of old shards Sanjay likes to collect for his museum. And I got a fright at first, the girl so wild-looking and stumbling about and I heard her gasp because the silly fool had walked into the edge of the reef. You may look great out here, Marina, my darlin', but you sure belong better in the Portobello Road.

'Holly,' the girl said. She took my arm. Her hand was cold and clammy. With her face ghostly white she was like a kind of zombie or one of those nasty things Tanty Grace can get to come up. There was a runway down the cheek where tears were going fast.

'Leave me alone, Mari,' I said. Then I looked closer at her

and I said, 'You was going to have shown a light here tonight, eh, Mari? You had a fall and lost the torch, eh?' I was annoyed at myself, I sounded like a nurse in an old movie or something. 'Time for a hot milk,' you might expect me to say next. And that's the funny thing with women, I guess, that even if one of them's digging up an arsenal of guns and the other's been raped on the way to set off the signal for an invasion that may change the shape of the balance of power with Cuba and Moscow and the States and all that, there's still something motherly, and daughterly too, in the way they carry on. Mari was clinging to me even harder now. I felt angry with her and sorry for her at the same time.

'Can't be bothered to get your hands dirty?' I said. And I shoved the spade at her. 'Go on – dig down a bit deeper and you'll strike something.'

But it was no good. The girl was pulling at me so hard I was reminded of poor crazy Pandora. We're to go back into the jungle and see where she dropped the torch, then? I said to myself because I was too furious to speak. That's a good way to spend Christmas Eve, Holly. Congratulations. And I saw Sanjay lying on top of her again and I could swear I heard the echo of her groans when she pulled me back into the trees. 'I'm coming, I'm coming,' I said and I stumbled after her. We'll have to go back to the house to get a light without being seen, I thought, but the very idea of seeing Sanjay covered in that swamp mud from his lie with the girl under the roots of the tree, made me cold all over.

I should have seen there'd be no sending off of signals then. I followed Mari, and I saw her go down the newly hacked pathway to the creek, and I saw her kneel. It was a horrible thing, it could have been Pandora there. Her words . . . it was like two halves of a splintered mind coming together and the pieces fit and make a picture . . . and the picture is different for each of them and yet it's the same. That mark . . . that white mark on Marina's neck, showing up there under that horrible great white moon . . . that red blotch on Pandora make her look like she cry all the time . . . the sudden rain that come down through the manchineel trees and bring poison-burn the day of the picnic at the lagoon.

Fear – and father – that was the part of the puzzle where the poor mad girl and Marina were joined. Fragments of fear, of envy and rage, of a mast sticking up in the creek's muddy water, and the sails of the new ship that Sanjay their father had made.

Millie's Letter to Her Daughter Mari

Me dear. You safe home now
since dem thunder claps
in darkness on verandah.
Dat corn-hair woman
come an take you, chile
an now you back to London.

You mine, chile.
London isn't like we
village dirt road, I know
Marina: it a swamp
of drain'-lan' what
grown a puzzle of streets
an' not one come to my door.

No time can touch one
mango season in di yard.
But Mari you can go
college all day long.
An' doctors free, chile.

ISLAND LANDOWNER SHOT DEAD IN US TROOPS' INVASION OF ST JAMES, GRENADINES

Sunday Times, 27 December 1983

James Allard, part-owner of the island of St James, Grenadines, is one of eight men reported to have been shot dead when US Marines made a surprise landing on the island. The landing took place at 1.30 a.m. on Christmas morning, sources in Barbados confirmed last night.

Information, understood to be reliable, of an expected invasion by members of Grenada's Marxist-Leninist New Jewel Movement suppressed by US forces in October, proved to be without foundation. Inhabitants of St James claim, however, that a small fleet of unlit fishing craft was sighted off the southern tip of the island and that the fleet turned back for lack of an expected signal. In the event, the arrival later of US Marines caused an exodus from the village to the lagoon in the extreme south. It is not known whether the villagers took the American troops for Grenadians when they saw the boats approach or whether the singing, dancing St Jamesians were simply celebrating the holiday in the traditional manner.

In the ensuing confusion, the Marines shot and mortally wounded eight men before the fact that their supposed opponents were unarmed could be brought home to them.

James Allard, forty-eight, had lived on St James for seventeen years. His lease on the southern half of the island was due to expire in the New Year.

Mighty Barby's Song

it woz in di expektashan
of a St James insohreckshan
dat we ran to Sanjay manshan
wen we check out di plan
but den wi see di lanlaad man
layin in di swamp head-doun

Tanty she mek mi andahstan
di men dem fire di aminishan
cos Yanki seh to kill Black man
but dem get di wrong impreshan
an kil a comrade in oppreshan

is Sanjay lie dere in concushan
di black mud it spread on he compleckshan